THE DISCOMBOBULATED DECIPHERERS

Julie Seedorf

Hermiony Vidalia Books

WELLS, MINNESOTA

Cheesecake recipe used with permission by *Taste of Home*. https://www.tasteofhome.com/recipes/peanut-butter-cup-cheesecake

Hermiony Vidalia Books
Printed in the United States of America
For more information, email hermionyvidaliabooks@gmail.com.

This is a work of fiction. Names, characters, places, and incidents are a product of the author's imagination. Locales and public names are sometimes used for atmospheric purposes. Any resemblance to actual people, living or dead, is completely coincidental.

Cover Design by Paula Ellenberger
www.paulaellenberger.com

The Discombobulated Decipherers/ Julie Seedorf. -- 1st ed.

ISBN-13: 978-0692971079
ISBN-10: 0692971076

This book is dedicated to those who hold the Christmas spirit in their hearts all year long. It is with that love that we will change the world.

[Handwritten inscription:]

Sue Ann

Look for the miracles of life... everyday,

They are there

[signature]

Acknowledgments

My granddaughter Maggie used her baking talent to help this
baking-challenged grandmother devise my recipes. She listened
to my vision for Jezabelle's yummy creations.
You are an inspiration to me.

To Annie Sarac at the Editing Pen, you are invaluable in editing
my work and making me look good.

I also want to thank my husband Mark who had infinite patience
with my writing fits and for helping me edit. He listened to me
read my entire book out loud! His insight was spot on.

Contents

Chapter One

Jezabelle slammed the door shut against the wind, keeping the blowing snow from swirling into the Brilliant Bistro. She brushed the snow off her clothes and rubbed her hands together trying to spark a little warmth into her cold fingers.

Looking around her new business, her face tried to break into a smile, displaying the happiness she felt, but her cold skin pulled tight as if it were ice trying to crack. Buying the bistro had been a good decision. She couldn't believe, at her age, she had made the choice to open her own business. And she couldn't believe Lizzy was foolish enough to become her partner.

Lizzy was Jezabelle's best friend and recently moved into Jezabelle's neighborhood. Not only were they business owners, they were now neighbors. She and Lizzy formed a friendship many years ago. Jezabelle kept Lizzy out of trouble, although Lizzy might say it was the other way around.

Glancing up at the lighted clock in the corner, she saw the glow of its numbers illuminating the seating area. She switched on the overhead light and navigated her way to the kitchen. Once there, she turned the soft lights in the kitchen on and turned the lights in the seating area off. If the citizens of Brilliant saw the light, they would assume she was open, and she hadn't put her cheesecakes and pies in the oven yet. Her

1

routine had been baking late at night in her home, but since she was now the owner of the bistro, she saw no reason her late nights couldn't be reserved for someone special instead of baking, hence the fact she was at the bistro at four a.m.

Lizzy was a night owl. Early mornings were hard for Lizzy, although when the Penderghast Puzzle Protectors investigated the puzzle the Brilliant brothers, founders of Brilliant, left for the community, Lizzy hadn't complained once about the early morning hours or the sleuthing at all hours of the day or night. It was natural for Lizzy to come in later in the day and stay until close at ten p.m. This gave Jezabelle the evening hours to herself.

The oven warmed while Jezabelle mixed muffin batter. She was ready to pop the batter into the oven when she heard a light tapping on the front door. She wiped her hands on a towel before peering through the opening between the kitchen and the seating area. Miranda Covington was the one making woodpecker sounds on the front door. Jezabelle gave the muffin batter one last glance before opening the oven door and sliding the muffins inside. Hurrying to the door, she let Miranda in.

"Miranda, what you doing out in this snowstorm? Although I know you are out and about at all hours of the night—but snowstorms? I guess I underestimated you."

"Jezabelle, I was coming to see if you needed any help. You know this is my best writing time, but I hit writer's block, so I thought I might see if you needed help with all the goodies you make. I love the snow, especially this time of year. The wind is terrible. It knocked the elf statue that is wrapped in Christmas lights over on its side in the square." Miranda stomped her feet to release the snow from her boots so she wouldn't track it into the bistro.

Jezabelle frowned. "There isn't an elf statue in Brilliant Square. There is the nativity scene and Santa's village, but the characters in the nativity scene and Santa and his elves are live people."

"But I saw him," Miranda insisted. "He was partially covered with snow, and I almost tripped over the little guy as I was coming through the park. I saw the lights first and was able to sidestep the statue."

"I am telling you, Miranda, there was no statue in the park yesterday," Jezabelle insisted.

"Is Santa missing any elves?" Miranda joked, following Jezabelle back into the kitchen.

"Santa may be missing." Jezabelle chuckled. "Phoebe was in the village yesterday volunteering to be Mrs. Santa Claus. Rumor has it Mrs. Claus heard about Phoebe and snatched Santa away in his sleigh."

Jezabelle checked the muffins in the oven.

"When will those muffins be done? I will prove it to you." Miranda stuck her chin out stubbornly, upset at not being believed.

"I have a few minutes before I have to get the Snowflake Dew Drops going. The cheesecakes just need to be cut before the first customers come in. The muffins have about fifteen more minutes to bake. Let's go and you can show me Mr. Elf Statue that doesn't exist." Jezabelle grabbed the coat she had thrown over the counter and also pulled on her knitted shawl and scarf.

Miranda was already waiting for Jezabelle by the door. She pulled the door open, and a gust of wind tried to blow the door shut again.

"It's a perfect Minnesota blizzard day. And you want to go out and find a tipped-over statue?" Jezabelle chided before shouldering her way through the door and out into the wind. "Good thing I kept my boots on."

"Isn't this fun?" Miranda commented. "It's beautiful in the dark with the Christmas lights on the light poles and the twinkling sparkles in the store windows. And... it's so peaceful because we are the only people on the street. We should sing."

"That would wake the dead, and then we'd have all kinds of noise. Where is this so-called elf statue? We're at the square."

Miranda pointed. "Over there, by Santa's village. See the lights on the ground?"

"This snow is almost as tall as me in places." Jezabelle kicked at the snow with her feet.

Miranda passed Jezabelle and stopped by the elf statue on the ground. "See, here it is."

Jezabelle leaned down and brushed the snow off the statue. The still figure was wrapped in Christmas lights that must have been run by a battery because they were not plugged into anything and they were still twinkling.

"I think we better call Hank Hardy," Jezabelle said, referring to the chief of police. "The elf's a statue all right, but he used to be Ernest the elf and one of Santa's helpers. We called him Twinkle Toes, but the only thing twinkling here anymore is the Christmas lights wrapped around his body."

Chapter Two

Yup, it's Ernest the elf." Police Chief Hank Hardy shook his head. "It looks like he has been here a few hours. How did you two discover him so early in the morning?"

"I was up early and decided to see if Jezabelle needed some help at the bistro, but first I took a little walk. I love the snow. I decided to visit the nativity scene, and that's when I stumbled on the statue or... um... I guess Ernest the elf. I thought he was a statue." Miranda leaned closer to get a better look at the stiff, wrapped in lights, making him a twinkling bundle.

"And I didn't walk by on my way to the bistro," Jezabelle added.

"Why didn't you use your underground walkway from Lizzy's house?" Hank asked.

"I didn't want to wake sleeping beauty." Jezabelle chuckled. "We need all the beauty sleep we can get. It's an age thing. Trust me."

The flashing lights of another police car interrupted their conversation. Stick Straight and Hanna Hardy joined them. Hanna was Hank's daughter.

"I had hoped we were done with dead bodies," Hanna said as she knelt down in the snow to take a closer look at the elf.

"Shouldn't we untangle him?" Jezabelle asked.

Miranda, being the mystery writer she was, said, "Jezabelle, you should know better. We can't disturb the scene of a crime until they finish processing it."

"Well, let's let them process it then. We need to get back to the bistro before we have black smoke coming from the roof and I have to serve smoked muffins to Red Hannahan. Instead of eating his muffins, he'll hose them down with his fire hose." She was referring to the fact that Red Hannahan was a firefighter.

Stick looked at Hank Hardy, a silent question in his eyes.

"Let them go," Hank said. "We know where to find them, and we can interrogate the witnesses over cheesecake later. Right now I think you're going to have to be crowd control."

Stick looked up to see more residents of Brilliant joining the scene. He quickly moved to block them. "Crime scene. Stay back."

"I can help you there," Jezabelle advised. Raising her hand, she yelled, "Free muffins at the Brilliant Bistro in five minutes."

Miranda grabbed Jezabelle's arm and started walking with her through the snow. "Are you crazy—free muffins? Do you have enough muffins?"

Jezabelle's face held a sly look. "No, but that's what I've got you for. I've got batter all made up. You bake while I interrogate. Someone must know what happened. And you know what they say, the criminal always shows up at the scene of the crime."

Jezabelle turned and yelled back down the street, "Free muffins, five minutes."

❄ ❄ ❄

"Why would someone murder Ernest the elf?" Miranda held open the door for Jezabelle.

"Maybe he stopped someone's kid from visiting Santa."

"Really? Jezabelle—you think someone would kill the elf for that reason?" Disbelief peppered Miranda's tone.

"You're the mystery writer, Miranda. Let's get those muffins. The rest of the batter is in the fridge. Start filling those muffin tins while I get the first batch out and cut the cheesecake."

The two women could hear the door opening and closing and chairs scraping across the floor. The buzz of conversation stopped when Jezabelle brought the muffins from the kitchen and set them on the counter. All eyes turned, waiting for her to speak.

"What? I know nothing. We just found poor old Ernest. There's nothing more to tell."

Miranda, still stirring muffin batter, joined Jezabelle at the bar. "She thinks he kept Santa from seeing someone's child."

"I do not. I just was trying to get you off the murder and back to the muffins. I know that mystery writer brain of yours, and it never quits, and I needed muffins." Jezabelle raised her hands in the air in a stop motion. "I don't think anyone murdered poor Ernest over their children."

The murmur of conversation started again.

Jezabelle rolled her eyes at Miranda. "You couldn't tell when I was joking? All we need is some parent being accused of knocking off Ernest because you were spreading rumors."

"Me?" Miranda shouted and then dropped her voice to a whisper when the room became silent and the bistro's customers turned their attention back to the two women. "Me? You're the one who accused a parent. Do you know what a mystery writer does with news like that? We twist it in our brains and internalize it, and then no one is safe."

The door opened and Hank Hardy and Jeb Jardine, Brilliant's other police officer, strolled into the restaurant. All conversation ceased as the crowd watched Hank and Jeb join Jezabelle and Miranda.

"Folks, it's too early in the investigation to have any news," Hank answered the crowd's silent question.

Jezabelle's neighbor, Mr. Warbler, looking like a rotund snowman dressed in an all-white snowmobile suit, hastened through the open bistro door to get out of the snow and cold. "I heard about the murder. Are we all in danger?"

The others again began mumbling to each other, asking the same question.

Jezabelle decided it was time to serve the muffins. "Who wants muffins and coffee this morning?" She grabbed the freshly brewed pot of coffee off the coffee maker while Miranda grabbed the cups, setting them down in front of their customers.

Hank Hardy and Jeb Jardine looked each other in the eye before Hank cleared his throat. "Again, it is too early in the investigation for us to have much information. All I can say is you need to be vigilant, and don't let this stop you from enjoying the festivity of Christmas."

"Did any of you see anything?" Jeb asked the crowd. Receiving no answer from the room of potential witnesses, he moved behind Hank Hardy and sat down on the barstool at the bar.

Turning to Jezabelle as she came back to the counter to get the muffins, he said, "Can you come over to the station and answer some questions, you and Miranda?"

The door opened again, and Lizzy and Phoebe Harkins entered the bistro. Phoebe was another of Jezabelle's neighbors in the Penderghast neighborhood. They too were part of the team of the Penderghast Puzzle Protectors when they banded together to solve the mystery and puzzle of their neighborhood.

"Lizzy, you're up early." Jezabelle acknowledged her best friend. "Do you think you Puzzle Protectors can watch the bistro for me? Warbler's already here, and Miranda has to come with me to the police station."

Lizzy's gasp could be heard throughout the restaurant. "We heard there was a murder, and that's why we came down. Are you okay? Did Miranda murder someone? You know I never did believe she only murdered people in her books."

"Ooh, she heard you, Lizzy. You weren't supposed to tell anyone. It was our secret that Miranda murders people and her books are just a cover-up for her murders. Now look what you've done. Miranda, you better call your lawyer." Jezabelle winked at Miranda.

"Jezzy, let's go." Hank Hardy and Jezabelle's friendship went way back to high school, and he was the only one Jezabelle allowed to call her Jezzy.

Miranda handed Jezabelle her coat. "We're off to the hoosegow. Don't burn down Jezabelle's bistro while we're gone."

"Let's go, Chief Hardy. Let the interrogation begin." Jezabelle let the snow blow in as she held open the door for Miranda and Chief Hardy. Turning back to Lizzy, she winked. "If we're not back by noon, you know the code for the jailbreak."

"Jeb Jardine, are you coming or are you official protection for Phoebe?" Chief Hardy asked.

Jeb quickly got up off the barstool and hurried out the open door, remembering Phoebe's flirtatious ways.

Hank laughed and followed Jeb out the door, closing it firmly behind him.

Chapter Three

Sadie Noir, the front-desk receptionist at the Brilliant Police Station, set the pot of coffee down in the middle of the table in the interrogation room. "We're going to have to add your names to our permanent cups because you visit so often." She chuckled, thinking of the past interrogations when Jezabelle and Miranda were trying to solve the puzzle and deaths in the Penderghast neighborhood.

"Yes, well… there must be something in the coffee to keep us coming back. Although maybe this terrible interrogation-room coffee is what makes your perps talk." Jezabelle smiled watching Sadie shut the door. Turning to Hank Hardy, she sweetly addressed the police chief. "What do you want to know Hank?"

"Wait, don't ask yet. I want to take notes for my next book." Miranda reached down and pulled a notebook and pen out of her purse. "With everything going on around this town, I don't have to make up stories for my writing."

Hank reached across the table and took the pen from Miranda. "I will be the only one taking notes here today. Now, Miranda, I would like you to take your coffee and go visit with Sadie. I want to talk to Jezabelle first."

"Remember to keep your story straight when it's your turn, Miranda. Don't implicate either of us. Do or die we'll stick together." Jezabelle cackled. "Hank, we already told you everything we know. No reason to send Miranda out. We don't know anything."

"That's for me to determine." Hank pointed to the door and waited until Miranda left before continuing. "How well do you know Miranda?"

Frowning, Jezabelle answered, "You don't suspect Miranda?"

"She was the one who found the body, and you must admit she is always out and about during the night."

"She's a writer. Writers keep crazy hours."

"She's a suspect until I can prove otherwise. What do you know about her?"

"Just what I've learned the past few months and I've surmised she is a great snoop and sleuth. She was crucial to us finding out what was happening in our neighborhood. Before that, none of us ever saw her because she was a reclusive writer. She doesn't talk much about her past."

"Jezzy, how did you happen to go to the square and find the body?"

"Miranda said someone tipped over the elf statue in the square. I knew there was no elf statue in the square, so I went with her so she could show me the statue."

"Did you know Ernest?"

Jezabelle shook her head. "Not really. He came in for goodies and hot chocolate once, but the Christmas season was just getting started, and as you know, he and Santa and the rest of the elves and the nativity scene were set up at the same time. By the way, who is Santa this year? I didn't recognize him. It's usually one of the firefighters, but they all were having coffee at the same time Santa was in the bistro the other day."

"Not sure, but I aim to find out. That's all for you. Send Miranda in when you leave. It looks like the snow is tapering off. Do you have a hot date tonight with your mysterious admirer?"

Jezabelle batted her eyelashes at Hank. "Is this part of the interrogation? If it is, I plead the fifth." Jezabelle opened the door. "Miranda, you're next. Sorry, I can't wait and keep an eye so they don't torture you some more with this coffee, but I have to get back to the bistro."

Hank rolled his eyes at the word torture as he held the door and indicated with a sweep of his arm that Miranda should join him.

Sadie waited until the door was shut before asking, "Did you tell him?"

"No, now wasn't the time. We have to wait for the right moment."

"And when will that be; it's getting close."

"I'll know. I have this inner sense of timing. Timing is such sweet sorrow you know." Jezabelle smiled.

Sadie's forehead crinkled. "No, I didn't know. Don't think I've heard that one.

"That's because it's a Jezzy Fezzy."

"I haven't heard that either. What does that mean?"

"Borrowing a quote from my niece, Delight Delure's friend, Granny, over in Fuchsia— you're on a need-to-know basis, and I'm the only one who needs to know."

Chapter Four

The wind wasn't blowing anymore when Jezabelle stepped outside the police station. Light snow drifted from above, highlighting the Christmas decorations on the light poles on Main Street. Down the road, Jezabelle saw flashing lights in front of her bistro.

What in the world? Fire trucks in front of the bistro? Jezabelle hurried toward the commotion.

The firemen were standing in front of the building, laughing.

"Red Hannahan, what is so funny about your trucks being in front of my bistro with your lights flashing?"

Another round of laughter answered Jezabelle's question before Red finally got his hilarity under control enough that he could speak. "That Warbler is always hanging around."

"Did he fall through my floor; I thought we had the floor problem under control?" She was referring to Warbler falling through his own bedroom floor.

"No, he decided he was going to put more Christmas lights up for you. He thought he could recreate a lighted tree on the roof."

"And then... and then"—Jet Pillager broke into laughter—"he decided to decorate your old chimney."

Red Hannahan interrupted Jet. "He decided to stand on top of the old chimney, and he lost his footing and fell in."

"He fell all the way down the old chimney to the fireplace? Good thing we don't use it because we are waiting to fix the chimney." Jezabelle looked up to the roof.

"No! I got stuck!" Mr. Warbler, seeing Jezabelle and the firefighters through the bistro window, came out the front door of the bistro and joined the group.

"Yup." Red Hannahan backed up the statement. "Half-in, half-out, just like the floor last time when you had your floor thief."

Warbler ignored the barb and said, "Jezabelle we need you inside." He grabbed her arm and pushed her through the door.

When they got inside, Jezabelle saw her noon help had come in. Hick Rafferty was in the kitchen, and Jezabelle could hear the sizzling of the grill as Hick performed his magic. Who knew her former garbage man would turn out to be a chef. When he needed a new job after almost losing his life moonlighting as a gravedigger, deciding garbage collection and grave digging were too dangerous, Jezabelle decided to give him a chance. It turned out that garbage wasn't his only game and grave digging wasn't going to be his only fame.

"This was left for you, Jezabelle." Karin Smedley, the noon waitress, handed Jezabelle a poinsettia."

Mr. Warbler stuck his nose over the plant, his eyes darting around looking at all sides of the living organism. "There's no card. Who's it from? You still haven't told us who is sending you these mysterious gifts?"

Jezabelle shrugged her shoulders. "No card, I guess. Maybe angels sent them. Put it on the bar; it will make a nice decoration." Turning to Warbler, she said, "Why did you haul me back inside? Can't take the heat from the firemen?"

Warbler indicated the table in the corner. Lizzy and Phoebe were sitting at the table staring at something in its center. "We discovered something."

Lizzy, seeing Jezabelle and Warbler, indicated they should join them. "We don't know what to make of this."

Pulling out a chair, Jezabelle sat down and looked at the object Lizzy had picked up from the center of the table. "It looks like a square of glass. What's so special about it?"

"We visited the murder scene, and we think it belongs to the murderer," Phoebe whispered.

"You were at the murder scene?" Jezabelle looked around the room to make sure no one heard her.

"Well, you and Miranda were hauled down to the police station, and we wanted to help," Lizzy explained.

"And you found this glass thing? It looks like a little glass block of ice." Jezabelle turned it over in her hand. The block was six-sided, about two inches by two inches.

Phoebe and Lizzy exchanged a glance.

"Well, not exactly at the murder scene," Lizzy said.

"No, nothing left at the murder scene except live people," Phoebe agreed.

Warbler pointed to the side that was now on top of the block in Jezabelle's hand. "Look what it says on it. It says Gasper."

"So?" Jezabelle questioned.

"And I found it on your roof, sitting on the top of your chimney. That's how I fell in. I saw it when I was putting up the Christmas lights. It was glinting in the snow. I climbed up to get it and fell in. I just made up the story of decorating the chimney to throw the fire crew off so they wouldn't tell Hank and the police department," Warbler explained.

Jezabelle counted to three, trying to be patient. "Would you mind telling me how this has anything to do with Ernest the elf? And how could you get into the crime scene? If this was on the chimney, on the roof of the bistro, how does that make it the property of the murderer?"

"Oh, it's not a crime scene anymore," Phoebe answered. "Santa and the other elves are back along with the nativity scene and the carolers. It's been cleared."

"And we didn't find anything," Lizzy added.

"Then we heard the fire trucks and came back over to the bistro to see what Hick might be burning down," Phoebe explained.

"When all the hoopla was over and I was rescued, I took them aside and showed them what I found, and Phoebe— being a wannabe mystery writer like Miranda—came up with a theory." Warbler nodded to Phoebe to continue.

"I think the murderer found this in the park and then when he was leaving the scene of the crime he passed by here. He took this little bauble, and thinking it wasn't worth anything, tossed it away up in the air, and it landed on your roof right by the chimney. We are so lucky it didn't get tossed down the chimney and get stuck."

Jezabelle stood up. "That's quite the theory. Since this landed on my roof, I guess we will add it to my Christmas décor. It could have been up there a long time or at least since Santa came down the chimney last year. Maybe it dropped out of his bag." She tossed the cube to Miranda who had just come in the door.

Miranda caught the cube in her hand. "Oh... I have one of these. I found it hidden in my basement in the base of the nativity scene that is carved into my basement stone wall. Mine says Balthazar."

Jezabelle looked from Miranda to the three back at the table. "Tonight—Miranda's house—ten p.m. Tell no one. Warbler, you might have just uncovered another Brilliant puzzle left to us by the ancestors. We'll let Hank and his police force find out what happened to Ernest the elf. We have to come up with another name for our little group activity since Hank made us promise to disperse the Penderghast Puzzle Protectors."

"You think these two little squares of glass lead to a puzzle?" Miranda relayed her skepticism as she tossed the glass cube in her hand.

"No, but we need an excuse to get involved in the murder investigation. So we have another puzzle whether we do or not." Jezabelle rubbed her hands together in anticipation.

"We have been warned to be careful by our chief of police," Miranda cautioned. "And he wasn't talking murderer on the loose. He said, 'No more Penderghast Puzzle Protectors. If there is any puzzle to be solved with this murder, the Brilliant police will put the pieces together. Your group is no more.'"

"Of course it is no more," Warbler agreed.

"Never again," Phoebe added.

"We aren't investigating the murder," Lizzy surmised.

"Balthazar would make a great character in my next mystery," Miranda added.

"It would, and we'll all be helping you write it tonight if Hank asks," Jezabelle cautioned.

A voice yelled from the kitchen, "Good thing this place is empty right now and only the ghost in the kitchen heard your plans. Is it true ghosts don't talk, just clang in the night?" Hick Rafferty slammed his cooking pots together, their sound ringing throughout the bistro.

Chapter Five

Miranda handed a glass of wine to each of her guests who were seated in her living room. "And to think all I used to do was write all the time, never having an idea I moved into such an interesting neighborhood."

"We had no idea we lived in a mysterious neighborhood either. It's amazing the rest of us have lived in Brilliant all this time without knowing about the Brilliant brothers' cleverness. You would have thought the ones that moved to Brilliant after the town was abandoned would have discovered its secrets before now." Jezabelle raised her glass. "To the brilliant Brilliant brothers for leaving us puzzled."

The others lifted their drinks to Jezabelle's toast, but Lizzy stopped with her hand in midair and said, "And to the residents of Brilliant who are so brilliant they didn't think to look for a puzzle even if they found a clue because they are into more brilliant things." She raised her glass to the toast.

Phoebe frowned. "Are you saying those that moved to Brilliant aren't brilliant?"

"No, I'm saying everyone is so smart they need things to make sense, and Jezabelle and the rest of us don't need things to make sense," Lizzy clarified.

"You are saying we aren't as smart as the others." Mr. Warbler glared at Lizzy, putting down his glass and stomping his feet in protest of her statement."

"Now Warby, don't get all upset." Lizzy grabbed his arm and batted her lashes at her neighbor. "We are smart, just not the kind of smart that doesn't think outside of the box. It is probably because none of us have ancestors born and raised in Brilliant. We are all transplants even if we have been here for many years."

"I'm not. I moved here when I was five and then left for a few years. Well... I guess that still makes me a transplant. Jezabelle went to high school here," Phoebe answered.

Jezabelle sipped her wine and listened to the verbal exchange. Finally she clanged a bell, one of Miranda's Christmas decorations sitting on the side table. "Let's get down to business before the wine tipples our thoughts."

"Did anyone ask Rock to join us?" Phoebe inquired.

Rock Stone was their neighbor and part of the Penderghast Puzzle Protectors until he wasn't.

"He's out of town," Jezabelle informed the group.

"Are you sure? I thought I saw him lurking by my bird feeders this morning," Warbler countered.

Jezabelle ignored Warbler and continued, "Now Miranda, let's see the little square of glass you found in your basement."

Miranda walked to the fireplace mantel, picked up her glass square, and held it up so they could see it. She pointed to wording carved on the outside. "See, it says Balthazar."

"And the other one we found says Gaspar." Phoebe dug into her pocket and pulled out the other glass cube.

"Well, we could change the name on the one cube to Jasper and then we'd have Gasper and Jasper." Mr. Warbler's rotund stomach moved up and down in waves, laughing at his own joke.

"There is really no reason why it is anything other than Christmas knickknacks and not a puzzle," Jezabelle reminded the others.

"But Miranda found one in her basement, and then one shows up on the roof of your bistro just as Ernest the elf is murdered? We have to investigate." Phoebe got up, pacing the floor while muttering, "We have to. We have to."

"Phoebe, calm down. What is your problem?" Lizzy's stern tone stopped Phoebe's pacing. Instead, Phoebe began to wring her hands. Then she sat down and broke into tears.

Phoebe was the tween in the neighborhood, younger than Jezabelle, Lizzy, and Mr. Warbler, but older than Miranda. She alternated between admitting her age was in the thirties or the forties, so they all decided to let her be whatever age she was comfortable with on any given day. It usually depended on what good-looking man was around for her to flirt with, and age made no difference to Phoebe. Plus somewhere she had acquired lots of money, and she wasn't averse to using her wealth to get her way.

Concerned, the group gathered around Phoebe. Jezabelle took Phoebe's glass and filled it with more wine, handing it back to the sobbing woman. "You really need a shot of whiskey to get it together, but this wine is going to have to do."

Phoebe grabbed the glass and swallowed it in one gulp before handing the glass back to Jezabelle, demanding, "More!"

Miranda sat down next to Phoebe. "Tell us what's wrong. You can't be upset over glass blocks."

Phoebe sniffed and lowered her eyes to the floor. "I'm not just upset about the blocks. There's something I didn't tell any of you."

"And what might that be?" Jezabelle asked.

"Ernest the elf"—Phoebe hesitated—"he was my date last night before he had to go to work."

"You were dating Ernest the elf?" Mr. Warbler plunked himself down in the rocking chair across from Phoebe.

Phoebe stood up. "Well, what of it. Just because he was shorter than me doesn't mean he wasn't charming."

"But he was new in town. No one knew who he was," Lizzy pointed out. "And you didn't say anything at the bistro to Hank to let him know that you had a relationship with Ernest."

"It wasn't a relationship!" Phoebe's uncharacteristic sharp tone startled all of them.

Softly Jezabelle asked, "Suppose you tell us what it was and what you aren't telling us."

Phoebe looked around the room, moved to the door as if to leave, and then slumped down in the chair next to the door. "Ernest just seemed to want to ply me with questions about Brilliant. He wasn't interested in me though he pretended he was. We went to dinner at the Brilliant BeDazzle Brewery, and when I realized he wasn't for me, I made an excuse and decided to leave. I walked past the town square to get my car because I left it in the Brilliant Bank parking lot. I kicked something in the snow, and it was this glass block."

Miranda interrupted. "The glass block was just lying in the snow?"

A red flush forming on her face, Phoebe shook her head. "Well, no. I... ah... was a little upset I even accepted the invitation from Ernest, and as I was walking past the church, I kicked at a tiny hole in the steps, and the cement crumbled a little, and I saw this thing in the hole when I bent over to rub my toe through my boots. I must have kicked it pretty hard. I dug out this small glass block. I examined it as I walked, and then I threw it on top of the Brilliant Bistro. I figured it was just a Christmas ornament some kid had tossed. I didn't intend it to stay on the roof; I just tossed it in my frustration."

"And you didn't think to tell me that before I climbed up on the roof to see what it was?" Warbler puffed.

"I wasn't there, remember? I was in the town square with Lizzy," Phoebe protested.

You didn't think to tell Hank Hardy that you knew Elfy and were with him last night?" Jezabelle chided.

"Well, you're going to get your chance now." Lizzy motioned to the window so they could see Hank Hardy walking up the sidewalk toward the door.

Chapter Six

Miranda opened the door before the police chief had the chance to ring the bell. "Chief Hardy, what are you doing here this late at night?"

Hank stepped in and stomped the snow off his boots. "I just happened to be patrolling the neighborhood, and I saw the lights. There were a few more questions I wanted to ask you, Miranda. And"—looking up and seeing the others in the room he continued—"I'm happy to see the rest of you are here too because I wanted to talk to all of you."

Frowning at his words, Jezabelle picked up an empty glass and motioned he should sit. "Do you want a glass of wine?"

Hank shook his head. "No, I'm still on duty. But I will take you up on that later when I get off. Oh... that's right, you have a secret admirer. I better not upset his apple cart."

"I don't think you came here to visit Miranda. I think you were driving through the neighborhood spying on me, Hank Hardy." Jezabelle teasingly winked at him.

Miranda interrupted the exchange. "What is it you wanted to ask me, Chief Hardy. I can't think I left anything out from this morning."

"Did you by chance notice if there were lights on in the church when you were on your way to the bistro?"

Miranda thought for a moment. "I honestly can't say. I had my head turned, tipped down, and I wasn't looking around because of the wind and snow. Did someone see lights on in the church? Was there another witness to Ernest's demise besides me?"

"That's all I wanted to know, Thanks, Miranda. If you think of anything else, you will let me know, won't you?" Hank ignored her question.

Mr. Warbler cleared his throat and looked at Phoebe. Phoebe glared back at Warbler.

"Something you wanted to say, Warbler?" Hank questioned.

"Something Phoebe wants to say," Jezabelle answered for Warbler.

Hank looked at Phoebe. "Phoebe?"

Phoebe squirmed in her chair. "Well... ah... I might have seen Ernest earlier before he became a statue in the park."

"May have?" Hank's eyebrows rose as he spoke.

Phoebe squirmed a little more. "Well, yes. I... ah... went out to dinner with him, but he wasn't my knight in shining armor, so I left him at the Brilliant BeDazzle Brewery. I didn't do it —I swear!"

"And you didn't tell me this earlier? Why?" Hank raised his voice in frustration.

"Hank, go easy on her. This is Phoebe. She doesn't think like the rest of us," Jezabelle pointed out.

"What? I don't think like the rest of you? What does that mean, Jezabelle?" Phoebe jumped up and approached Jezabelle.

"Settle down, Phoebe. It just means your mind was on something else, like putting puzzles together." She winked at Phoebe.

Phoebe stood up straighter, thought a minute, and then said, "Oh, yes, that's right."

"Speaking of puzzles," Hank added, "remember the Penderghast Puzzle Protectors do not exist anymore. The puzzle in your neighborhood is over, and you will not get involved in Ernest the elf's sad demise. Do you understand? Immerse yourself in the Christmas pageant at the church. I hear all of you are involved in that. It should keep you out of trouble. Do you understand?"

"Yup," Warbler chirped.

"Um hmm," Miranda mumbled, keeping her head lowered.

"'Silent Night.' We will concentrate on 'Silent Night,'" Phoebe chimed in.

"And did you hear we are doing a Valentine Service too on Valentine's Day?" Jezabelle countered.

"Oh, that's nice, Jezabelle," Lizzy replied, not answering Hank's order.

"I've got to be going. Phoebe, can you come down to the station in the morning so I can ask you some more questions. I will visit the Brilliant BeDazzle Brewery and see if they can confirm what you just told me."

"Sure," Phoebe answered.

Jezabelle followed Hank to the door. "Oh and Hank, you might want to talk to Pastor Sifter about the Christmas pageant. I think he has something he wants to ask you."

"Bye, Jezabelle, don't stay up too late unless it is for a date."

"You rhyme. Have you been dating someone in Fuchsia? I hear that Granny over there is teaching the entire community to talk in rhyme. She chuckled as he gave her a confused look before walking out the door.

"Jezabelle, weren't you supposed to be the one to ask Hank, not the Pastor?" Mr. Warbler questioned after making sure Hank wasn't on the porch listening at the door.

"I didn't exactly say I'd ask him. I told Sadie Noir and her committee I would see to it. I just did. I saw that Hank asked Pastor Sifter. Enough about that, let's get back to business."

"What business?" Phoebe asked. "We don't know if we have any business. We just have two glass cubes, and we have been told to stay out of Ernest's demise."

"Well, not exactly. We have been told the Penderghast Puzzle Protectors are no more, but he didn't say anything about the Discombobulated Decipherers."

Chapter Seven

I'll have some of that luscious cheesecake and a brew of Christmas caramel coffee."

Jezabelle turned from cutting her cheesecake to see whose voice was ordering her goodies. "Why, Santa, we haven't officially met. I'm Jezabelle Jingle."

With a twinkle in his eye, the man with the rotund figure, red suit, and sporting a real gray beard and tufted eyebrows, reached out his hand to touch Jezabelle's, whose hands were resting on the counter in front of him. "Ho, ho, ho, I know who you are. Santa knows all. And Santa loves his jingle bells."

Peering into his face to see if she could tell if the town square Santa was one of the firemen, she answered, "Yes, well, let me guess. You aren't Red Hannahan or Cliff Rainy—wrong color eyes."

Laughing, the big man answered, "I told you, I'm Santa. Let's just leave it at that. I'm not from around here. I heard at the North Pole there was an opening and Brilliant needed a Santa, so I flew in early. I have to be back early on Christmas Eve day to help my elves pack my sleigh."

"Okay, Santa, I'll play along." She turned back and put a slice of Red Candy Cane Cheesecake on a plate and set it in front of him. "I'll be back after getting your coffee." She gave him another hard look, trying to figure out his identity.

Hick watched the exchange from the kitchen and teased Jezabelle when she came into the kitchen to check her Red Ribbon Sprinkle Cupcakes still in the oven. "A little flirty with Santa there aren't you? Trying to get in good with the big guy so he'll bring you an extra Christmas present?" Hick laughed.

"Do you suppose he knows anything about Elfy's murder?" A faraway look entered Jezabelle's eyes.

"Say, Jezabelle Jingle, is he your secret admirer? You have to spill soon who is always leaving you notes and cute little gifts and flowers." Hick ignored her question.

Giving Hick the evil eye, she said, "Go out there and deliver his coffee, and ask him if he knew Ernest the elf very long? See if he knows anything. See if you can figure out who he is."

"You can't do that? I got in enough trouble before, and I didn't even know there was trouble," Hick reminded her.

"I can't risk it. Hanna Hardy is sitting at a booth, talking to a woman I don't recognize. Even when she's off duty her deputy's brain is always working, and she'd tell Hank."

"If I end up in another grave, it's on you," Hick warned.

"And ask if he ever notices lights on in the church at night."

"Do you want me to ask where Mrs. Claus is too?"

Jezabelle's face crinkled into a smile. "No, give it a few days. I am sure Phoebe will be looking for that information."

Jezabelle busied herself pouring coffee and chatting with the other diners as Hick talked to Santa. She had just finished pouring Mr. Ellery's coffee when she heard a thud on the counter. Turning in the direction of the unexpected noise, she saw Santa pick up his hand from where he brought it down to pound the counter. He stood up, turned, and quickly exited the bistro. She hurried over to Hick, who was standing, staring at the closed door.

"What did you say to him?" she asked.

"Everything was fine until I asked him about lights at the church at night. He got very agitated, brought his hand down hard on the counter, and then left. I have no idea. Maybe he is tired of all the questions."

"Did he know Ernest very well?"

Hick shook his head. "He said he just met him when he came to Brilliant to get the feel of the town's wishes for Christmas."

"That's a strange way to put playing Santa."

The door of the bistro opened again, and Phoebe flounced in, a mischievous smile on her face.

"Well, your interrogation at the police station must have gone well. You look like the cat that swallowed the canary," Jezabelle remarked.

Phoebe sat down at the counter. "I just met Santa. He is very charming. And he didn't bring Mrs. Claus with him. He left her at the North Pole." She giggled.

"And are you in the clear with the police for not telling them about your date with Ernest?" Jezabelle asked.

"Yes, I had a stalker that night and didn't know it. He cleared me."

"A stalker?" Hick commented. "The police must have him in custody if he cleared you."

"My stalker was Pastor Sifter. He was walking back to the parsonage behind the church from checking the nativity scene to make sure all the lights were shut off and the live Mary and Joseph and Wise Men didn't leave any scenery items out. He saw me kick the concrete stairs. In fact, he went over after I continued on my way to check to see what I had kicked. He told Hank the steps are starting to crumble from age and they are going to have to be replaced. I wonder what else they'll find under the steps. They aren't going to repair them until spring."

"Hank talked to Pastor Sifter then. Did Hank say anything about Pastor Sifter asking him?" Jezabelle's face held a hopeful look.

Phoebe shook her head. "I don't think he said a thing. Hank said he asked Pastor Sifter about the Christmas pageant, and Pastor Sifter said Sadie had talked to you about it and you would talk to him."

"That's confusing," Hick commented.

"Don't you have to get back to the kitchen? The noon crowd will be coming in," Jezabelle reminded him.

Hick winked. "You're losing your flirting skills, Ms. Jezabelle. When I was a garbage man, you would have thought of another way to get me to mind my own business." He laughed and retreated to the kitchen.

Jezabelle felt a brush on her ankles. She looked down to see Mr. Shifty, the cat that had adopted her earlier in the year, rubbing around her ankles.

Reaching down, she picked him up. "How did you get here Mr. Shifty? It's cold for you to be wandering outside. I thought I left you sleeping by my fireplace."

"You did," Lizzy, coming through the door from the basement, remarked. "I stopped over to your house and let myself in with the key. I forgot my appointment book in your living room the other day when we were going over our schedule for the bistro. Mr. Shifty dashed out when I opened the door and ran over to Rock's house. I think he was lonely, so I decided to bring him along. I came through the tunnel from my house so Mr. Shifty wouldn't get any colder."

"We haven't got Brilliant's rule changed about having animals in restaurants yet. Never thought I'd admit it, but Fuchsia might have had a good idea allowing animals in all businesses." Jezabelle picked up Mr. Shifty.

"You can bring him to the basement with us. I've got some ideas about what we can do with it to rid us of the memory of our encounter down there and also to utilize the space better. We need to find an architect to tell us if it's possible to do some remodeling so this old building doesn't fall down on top of us."

Jezabelle followed Lizzy down the steps, keeping a tight hold on Mr. Shifty so he didn't get away.

The basement of the bistro held a small kitchen on one end and old shelving that used to hold the flour and some other unsavory illegal things when Jiffy Jacks owned the building. The shelves still held the flour and baking products that Jezabelle and Lizzy use to make the tempting morsels they baked. On one side was the door that led to the tunnel that Baxter Brilliant had built so he could get to the bistro in the wintertime, although back then it was a pharmacy or drugstore.

"This place is kind of dusty and rugged." Jezabelle pointed to the wood flooring joists on the ceiling. "Maybe we can hang a ceiling down here and use this basement space for something other than storage."

Lizzy clomped back up the old wood steps that were unfinished wood and tapped the door to the upstairs of the bistro. "This door is authentic." The old basement door, built out of plain, unfinished old wood fit right in with the roughness of the unfinished basement.

Jezabelle moved over to the window on a wall near the kitchen sink. It was a regular rectangular old basement window. The casing was worn and rotting in a few places. As she moved the curtain aside, she said, "It is not a legal window. If we remodel, we will have to replace it. But I thought this space could be added to our dining. Maybe we could call it the Cave and use it at night for our dining with the wine and keep the upstairs a coffeehouse day and night. It would have ambiance down here. A wine cave and we could also host private parties."

"We could make it an egress window so it was legal, and put those cute little glass blocks in it like they have at the Brilliant Bank in their basement windows, but somehow we would have to have it have it open to keep up to code. Those windows are bigger than these. I think they are original. We could replicate the old bank windows, keeping the history of the building." Lizzy joined Jezabelle by the window.

"I wonder if we can find out more about the history of this building at the Lackadaisical Meanderings Library. Now that Miranda has been appointed temporary administrative book guru until they find someone else qualified to take Marion's place, maybe she can sift through the records and find an original picture of the building." Jezabelle moved to the shelving and continued, "I will be sorry to tear down these shelves. What will we do for storage?"

"We can build a little storage room in front of the door to the tunnel. That way we won't have any customers trying to snoop and end up surprising me at my house." Lizzy laughed. "I think we've had enough surprises lately."

"Jezabelle! Jezabelle!" Hick's voice drifted down the stairs from the kitchen of the bistro.

"Down here, Hick," Jezabelle answered.

Hick's loud laughter muffled his voice when he said, "Up here, Jezabelle. This is too big to bring down to you. Your secret admirer has struck again."

Chapter Eight

I'm your best friend and you can't tell me who your secret admirer is?" Lizzy protested.

Jezabelle ordered, "Lift and turn."

"It's a good thing I have a van"—Mr. Warbler puffed—"or you wouldn't have got Mr. Rudolf home. Who gave you this thing anyway?"

"Push," Lizzy ordered.

"It's too wide," Warbler answered.

"Wait—maybe the head turns." Jezabelle grabbed the head of the huge stuffed reindeer and turned it so it wasn't blocking the large body they were trying to get through the door."

A click and a flash lit up the darkening night.

Jezabelle turned in the direction of the flash, and another one went off in her face. "Snoop Steckle, you nosy nelly reporter, what do you think you are doing?"

"I heard we had a new romance in town and you were sent a note along with a large endearing gift, and it's been a slow news day. No murders today so I thought I would stake out your house to see what the hubbub was all about. Would you like to make a statement?"

Jezabelle turned back to the door. "Push," she ordered her friends.

Mr. Warbler laid his large body right up against the fluffy tail of the stuffed animal and shoved at the same time Lizzy pushed the legs closer together so it would wedge through the door.

Jezabelle stood behind Warbler and pushed on him. All three fell through the door after the giant stuffed reindeer. The reindeer landed in the middle of the room while the three cohorts landed in front of the door. Jezabelle turned and slammed the door shut in Snoop Steckle's face.

They heard a yowl.

Frowning, Lizzy said, "That doesn't sound like Snoop."

The door flew open and almost hit Mr. Warbler.

"What the heck is that?" Phoebe demanded.

Before Jezabelle could answer, Jasperine, Phoebe's dog formerly known as Jasper, and Max, Mr. Warbler's big hound, bounded into the room pouncing on the reindeer. As Phoebe reached for the dogs, they heard a loud meow, and Mr. Shifty and Mrs. Mysterious jumped on top of the dogs.

"Well, I guess Mr. Shifty decided he didn't like waiting in the van," Jezabelle remarked.

"Or Mrs. Mysterious led him astray." Lizzy chuckled.

The three got up off the floor and shooed off their furry creatures.

"You still didn't answer me," Phoebe asked as she examined the reindeer. "This thing is big. Why in the world would you buy something like this?"

"She didn't," Mr. Warbler remarked.

"No, her secret admirer sent it to her. Here––read." Lizzy thrust a note into Phoebe's hands.

"Here's a deer, just for you. Keep him near, don't be blue. You're a dear, just like Boo." Phoebe's face crinkled. "Not much of a poet. Who's Boo?"

Mr. Warbler indicated the tag around the reindeer's neck. "Boo is the reindeer. Who ever heard of calling a reindeer Boo?"

"That's enough. As long as we are here, let's have a little cheesecake. I happen to have some in the fridge, and we can talk about our plan." Jezabelle headed to the kitchen.

Warbler turned to Lizzy. "Plan, we have a plan?"

Lizzy batted her eyes at Warbler. "Oh Warby, we always have a plan. We just don't know what it is yet."

Chapter Nine

The next morning, Lizzy flounced into the bistro as Jezabelle and Hick were conferring about the evening dinner and wine selection for the late afternoon transition to a wine bar.

"Jezabelle, let's walk down to the bank and take a look at their basement windows before I get mired in the bistro business."

"You're window shopping at the bank?" Hick teased. "Looking for a rich banker to flirt with?"

Jezabelle swatted Hick with a hot pad. "No... we are looking at remodeling the basement so we can move the wine part of our business downstairs."

"Windows and wine ain't that fine." Hick laughed.

Jezabelle swatted him again, playfully, before taking off her apron, exchanging it for her winter coat.

"Then we need to stop by the nativity scene at the town square," Lizzy informed Jezabelle as they were walking out the door.

"And we would do that why?"

"To save Joseph."

Jezabelle stopped and looked at Lizzy. "Joseph, as in Mary and Joseph?"

"Yes, Phoebe is over there flirting with Joseph. She offered him a room in her house."

"Maybe we need to send her mother over there," Jezabelle suggested.

"Phoebe's forty years old. I don't think her mother has that much influence on her."

"She's forty?" Jezabelle frowned. "I always forget we don't really know her age; she's just a youngster compared to us."

"And a rich one too. She has never told us how she got all that money. Her mother doesn't seem to have money. In fact, I heard Phoebe pays all her mother's expenses."

"We're here." Jezabelle stopped in front of the large basement window of the bank.

"Isn't this beautiful? All these small glass squares. They remind me of the two squares of glass we found." Lizzy squatted down and brushed the snow away from the window where the glass met the sidewalk. "Look."

Jezabelle leaned down and put her face close to the glass square where Lizzy was pointing. "It looks like there is something etched in this bottom corner piece. I need a spyglass to see what it says."

"I can't make it out either. Do you suppose our glass squares were once part of a window?"

Jezabelle ran her hand over the glass. "Maybe."

"Jezabelle, Lizzy, what are you doing out here in the cold and snow and on the ground? Did you slip on the ice?" Hutchinson Bellamy, the bank president, came out of the building and, seeing the women, stopped to investigate. He reached down to help both the ladies off the ground.

"No... we were looking at your window. We are going to do some remodeling over at the bistro and want to put in a basement window just like this but one that opens," Jezabelle explained.

"Well, I'm not sure these are original, but they are very well preserved. You know you might be able to get Tom Burnside over at Intellectual Icycles to replicate them. He has been tinkering with custom windows lately, so when Icicle business is slow, he has something to keep him busy.

"Good idea. We will check with him. Thanks, Hutch." Jezabelle used his nickname, having known him since they were kids.

"We have to be going. Joseph needs us to rescue him from Phoebe." Seeing Hutch Bellamy's confused look she said, "Long story. Are you coming to practice for the Christmas pageant tomorrow night?"

"I am." Turning to Jezabelle, he questioned, "Have you asked Hank yet?"

"Me, ask Hank? I thought you were going to ask Hank."

Hutch's face crinkled up in washboard wrinkles. "Me? I'm supposed to ask Hank?"

Jezabelle nodded her head. "Why yes, don't you remember? You better get on it. Come on, Lizzy, we better rescue Joseph." She grabbed Lizzy's arm and pulled her down the street.

"You were supposed to ask Hank," Lizzy reminded her.

"No... Pastor Sifter was supposed to ask Hank."

Lizzy shook her head vehemently. "No, I remember distinctly it was you."

A sly smile spread across Jezabelle's face. "Well, now Hutch thinks he's the one to pop the question, so let's just let him think that so he asks Hank."

"There's Phoebe now. And it looks like we are just in time. Joseph looks rattled; Mary is trying to shield them from the crowd. It's a good thing they don't have the baby Jesus there yet since it's not Christmas, or he would be crying." Lizzy hurried ahead of Jezabelle to get to Phoebe.

Jezabelle veered off to the side, waving at Santa and the elves as she passed and grabbed the line tethering the cow to the stake at the side of the nativity scene. "Come on, Bossy. You are going to meet Phoebe."

The crowd around the nativity moved aside for Jezabelle and Mrs. Bossy. "Joseph, Mrs. Bossy here needs to be fed. Can you take her down to Lurches Livery and feed her?" She brought the cow right in between Phoebe and Joseph. She could hear Mary heaving a sigh of relief.

"Yes, Joseph please tend to our livestock," Mary said, staying in character. "Our baby will be born soon and will need the warmth from our beast and for her to provide milk for us."

Joseph grabbed the cow and, still flustered by Phoebe's attention, pulled the cow right into Phoebe, knocking her into the shepherd standing nearby. They both fell to the ground, arms and legs tangled together.

The shepherd looked into Phoebe's eyes and said, "I think I fell for you. Would you like to help me tend my sheep tonight?"

Phoebe quickly extracted herself from the shepherd's arms. Flustered, she stood up before answering, "And become one of your flock, I think not!"

The shepherd winked at her and extended a hand indicating she should help him up.

Phoebe swatted the hand away and said, "Sigfried Shepherd, I am on to your flirtatious ways, remember? I don't know what you are doing here pretending to be a shepherd when you are a wolf. I have been part of your flock, and you didn't tend it well." Turning away, she stomped through the snow to the other side of the square.

The shepherd stood up and, seeing Jezabelle and Lizzy's astonished stares, remarked, "Apparently, she had a sheepish experience," before turning back and taking his place in the nativity scene

"Should we go after her?" Lizzy whispered to Jezabelle.

Jezabelle shook her head. "No, we accomplished saving Joseph. But who knew the real point of the flirting was the wolf in shepherd's clothing."

Miranda was waiting for them when they got back to the bistro. They found Hick sitting next to Miranda in a booth, both of them engrossed in conversation over something lying on the top of the table.

"What do you have, Miranda, that is distracting our chef?" Jezabelle leaned over the top of the booth and peered over the top of their heads at the paper they were studying, while Lizzy sat down opposite them in the booth.

"It's a picture of the outside of this building back when it was first built. I found a stash of old pictures of the buildings of Brilliant hidden under one of the display cases in the library. I decided to rearrange the Brilliant Brother's Memorial Room because I thought we could add to the history with our last find. But I was only able to snatch this picture away before I was replaced as the temporary librarian."

"You were replaced?" Lizzy asked.

"I was. Something about the board not liking my moving the Brilliant brothers furniture around and... also they accused me of spending too much time reading and not enough time cataloging. I mean, shouldn't every good librarian know what books to recommend, and how could I do that if I hadn't read them?"

"Good point," Jezabelle agreed. "So what do we need to do to bring the outside back to its former beauty?"

"Not much." Hick pointed to the picture. "Look at this. There was an outside alleyway entry to the building and the basement. See this railing. There were open steps outside leading down to the basement, and it appears to be right where your window is. Maybe there was a door there."

Jezabelle studied the picture. "It's too bad those stairs aren't there anymore. They must have filled it all in and closed the door when putting in the basement window. It would have made it perfect for a separate entrance for us to separate our wine bar and our coffeehouse. We wouldn't need to convert it every night. We could run both all afternoon and evening."

"I wonder why a pharmacy or drugstore would need a separate entrance like that," Miranda mused.

"Well, Ms. Mystery writer, put your nose to being nosy and find out." Jezabelle nudged the writer.

Hick smiled. "I'll help you. It's too bad the Penderghast Puzzle Protectors are no more, at least that's what I heard from Hank Hardy and Hanna, because I'd love to join."

The three women shared a glance. Jezabelle nodded.

Miranda gave Hick a conspiratorial smile. "Well, can you keep a secret?"

Chapter Ten

Jezabelle was twirling her wine around in her glass when she heard a knock on her door. She looked at the clock on the wall. It was eleven p.m. She wasn't expecting her secret visitor tonight. She wondered who else would be knocking on her door so late.

"Jezabelle?" Mr. Warbler's voice could be heard on the other side of the door.

She set her wineglass down, straightened her Mickey Mouse robe, and shuffled her feet, which were ensconced in alligator-style slippers, over to the door. "Warbler, what are you doing here at this time of night? Everyone okay?"

Giving her a sheepish look, he said, "Well, I saw your lights when I was coming back from my studio, and I know occasionally you keep later hours staying up baking. I thought maybe you might like to come over and have a glass of wine. I want to talk to you about something but not when Lizzy is with you, and lately you two seemed joined at the hip."

Jezabelle opened the door farther, indicating he should come in. "Why don't we have our glass of wine here since I was enjoying a late-night swig."

Mr. Warbler entered the living room. "You and the others in the Penderghast... uh... I mean the Discombobulated Decipherers know my little secret, so I know I can trust you."

Jezabelle handed him a glass of wine. "Sit down and we will chat. It can stay between us. How is your painting going?"

Mr. Warbler was really the renowned painter Marco Renaldo, but no one in Brilliant was aware of his identity except those in their puzzle group, having discovered it when they were investigating the secrets they found when there were floornappers active in Brilliant.

"It is going fine. I am painting Phoebe's mother again. To be honest, I think she likes me. Don't tell Phoebe. I haven't figured out what to do about her yet. She doesn't know who I am, just the talented neighbor of her daughter."

"Has she told you anything about Phoebe, such as how Phoebe became so rich?"

Warbler shook his head. "No, not a word. I'm not sure she knows."

"Does the reason you wanted to talk have to do with Phoebe's mother?"

Warbler hesitated. "No, I want to talk about Lizzy. Do you think she would let me take her to dinner and court her?"

Jezabelle laughed. "That is an old-fashioned term I haven't heard in a long time. I think looking for clues about the Brilliant brothers has set you back away from the fine art of dating in this century. You know, Warbler, Lizzy doesn't call you Warby for nothing. It's like a pet name."

"So has she said anything that might make you think I have a chance?"

Jezabelle shook her head. "If she did, I couldn't tell you. She's my best friend, and I couldn't break her confidence."

Mr. Warbler hung his head. "I understand. I have to respect that. Why is it you never married, Jezabelle?"

Jezabelle was quiet for a moment before answering, "I'll let you in on a little secret. Even Lizzy doesn't know this one, and she's been around in my early years. I was married for all of two weeks when I was nineteen."

Mr. Warbler's mouth dropped open. "What happened? Two weeks isn't a long time."

Jezabelle's eyes took on a faraway look. "It wasn't meant to be, but I will tell you this. I never married because I never found anyone I loved as much as him. And if you breathe a word of this, I will shout to the world that you, Marco Renaldo, live in Brilliant and you are in love with Phoebe's mother. It wouldn't take long for Phoebe to take you out. She's pretty protective of her mother, and so is her sister."

Mr. Warbler laughed. "Jezabelle, I know you wouldn't do that, but your secret is safe with me. I hope you'll tell me more at some point in time."

Jezabelle nodded her head. "We will see, and good luck with Lizzy. I think you two would be adorable together."

Mr. Warbler handed Jezabelle his wineglass and moved to the door. "Good night and we'll see you tomorrow night or should I say tonight at Christmas practice. Did you ask Hank?"

Chapter Eleven

Jezabelle was getting ready to leave for the bistro when her phone rang. It was four a.m. First Warbler showed up at eleven p.m., and now Lizzie was calling. Usually at this time of morning, Lizzy was still snuggled warmly in her bed having worked the late shift at the bistro.

"Lizzy, is something wrong?"

"The bank window was smashed last night in a case of vandalism. The only reason I know is that Hanna woke me up wanting to know if I saw anything when I got off work at the bistro."

"Did you?" Jezabelle asked.

"No, but I was at the scene of the crime right before it must have happened."

"Why were you walking home at that time of night? I know Brilliant is safe, but it's cold out and Ernest the elf was turned into a Christmas statue," Jezabelle pointed out.

"No, I had my car, but I also had my spyglass—you know, my magnifying glass—so I stopped by the bank on the way home to check out the corner glass in the basement window. I used my cell phone as a flashlight."

"Were you able to see what was scratched on the glass block?"

"I was. It was Melchior."

45

"Melchior?"

"Yes, and that would make sense. I did some research on the internet after I got home. I typed in all three names, and they are the names of the Three Wise Men or the Magi of Bethlehem."

Jezabelle, deep in thought, hesitated before answering. "Well, we thought the glass blocks might be Christmas decorations since Miranda found hers wedged in a wall in a nativity scene in her basement. And the other was tucked away under the church steps, and it might have been there for a long time. We should have known those were the names of the Three Wise Men. But why would the Brilliant brothers hide glass blocks with the Wise Men's names? It must be another puzzle, but it is strange that we are the ones finding this after all these years. No one as snoopy as Miranda lived in her house. The last person who lived there was old and crabby and didn't change a thing, and she lived there for at least a hundred years."

"A hundred years. I think you are embellishing," Lizzy chided.

"Well it seemed like a hundred years after I moved in and I had to deal with her. Although I am sorry she had to leave the way she did."

"What does that mean?"

"One day a car pulled up and they helped her into the car, and she has never been seen again. Soon afterward the house was put up for sale, and that is when Miranda moved in," Jezabelle explained.

"Interesting... and the steps fell apart at the right time, and we wouldn't have noticed the bank window if we were not going to remodel. By the way, it was the basement window that was smashed."

"Did they break the glass block?" Jezabelle asked.

"I don't know. I didn't think to ask. My brain is a little sleepy. Do you think Ernest the elf's murder has anything to do with the glass blocks? Maybe we should tell the police department about our find."

"It's all a mystery at this point. I wouldn't know what the glass blocks have to do with Ernest. We need to see if we can track down some of those puzzle books under the name Roosevelt Strong since that was the name the brothers used when they published them. The books have to be somewhere. Maybe we need to check some antique stores and be on the lookout for them."

"Yes, there is no carved map this time, or least if there is, we haven't found it. Have you seen Rock Stone lately? I miss his slow drawling help," Lizzy added.

"Warbler thought he saw him hanging around the bird feeders the other day, but Hanna says he is out of town. Oh... look at the time. I have to get to the bistro. Get some sleep and we'll see you at rehearsal at the church."

"I will, and since we decided to close tonight so Hick and I can go to rehearsal, it will be an early evening. See if you can get Hank to tell you whether the square got smashed too," Lizzy suggested.

"Why don't you call Warbler and have him pick you up for rehearsal since you don't have to work. I'll call Miranda and Phoebe, and we can meet after rehearsal at Phoebe's for some snacks and a drink."

"I can drive myself, and then you and I can come home together and chat about who we need to contact to look at the basement and see if the building is stable enough for our remodel," Lizzy suggested.

"Ah... I can't tonight. Warbler's a little down and could use some cheering up. And if my plans change, I can always catch a ride back home with you. I have one more question. Why are we calling ourselves the Discombobulated Decipherers? None of us seem to know."

Jezabelle thought for a minute. "I'll explain it tonight when I figure it out. I just liked the name." The line went dead in her hand. Jezabelle looked at her phone. "I guess she didn't like the answer."

Chapter Twelve

Jezabelle stood in front of the Brilliant Bank, snow spitting tiny drops of moisture onto her hair. The smashed window was boarded up. It was still early in the morning, but she could see through the darkness little shards of glass, twinkling up from the cracks between the sidewalk and the building. Shining the flashlight from her cell phone into the cracks of the sidewalk, it was hard to decipher the difference between the crystal snow and the glass.

Shaking her head, she moved on down the street to the Brilliant Bistro to put in her first morning baked goods. It would soon be six a.m., and her early-morning customers would want their coffee and sweets to fill their tummies before they went to work. She left her smart car parked in front of the bank.

"HH, what are you doing in front of my business so early in the morning?"

"I thought I'd have some coffee and donuts before I headed home for a few hours of sleep. We had a little excitement here last night."

Hank Hardy moved aside so Jezabelle could unlock the door of the bistro.

"I heard that. Lizzy called me this morning. Was someone trying to break in and rob the bank?"

"No, it appears it was just some prankster. Probably some kids, although they smashed part of the window and then seemed to chip away and remove the rest of the blocks one by one. We had smashed glass with the blocks stacked on top of one another as if a little kid was playing with them." Hank sat down at the bar.

Jezabelle started the coffee and went into the kitchen and turned on the ovens. She pulled out the cinnamon rolls that had been rising in the oven and touched them gently to make sure they were the way she wanted them. She plopped them back in the oven before returning to the bar to talk to Hank.

"Did you find any blocks with etching on them?" she asked.

Hank shook his head. "No, I don't think so. Why do you ask? We have them over at the station for evidence and to see if we can lift any fingerprints."

The door opened, and Hank's daughter, Hanna, and Stick Straight entered the bistro, saving Jezabelle from answering. Seeing her dad, Hanna made a beeline for the stool next to him. Stick sat down on the other side of him.

"We have a report of the lights being on for a short time in the middle of the night at the church again," Hanna said.

"Just like the night of Ernest the elf's murder," Stick reminded them.

"Who saw them?" Jezabelle quizzed.

"Rock. He got home late last night. He wasn't aware of all the happenings around here or that Ernest was murdered," Hanna explained.

"Where is Rock now? I need to talk to him." Jezabelle threw the words over her shoulder as she poured coffee for the newcomers.

"Gone," Hanna answered.

"Gone where?" Jezabelle set the coffee in front of Hanna.

"Just gone. I don't want to talk about it." Hanna's face screwed up in a stubborn pose as if she were gluing her lips shut.

"Let's change the subject," Hank suggested.

"But...," Jezabelle sputtered.

Stick Straight decided to change the conversation. "We need to interview Pastor Sifter and his wife, Nellie, to see if they left the lights on in the church this time since they didn't know anything about it before."

"Whoops. I smell the cinnamon rolls." Jezabelle hurried into the kitchen. She could hear the other three whispering to each other.

The door opened again, and the firefighters came in along with Fleck Flaherty, owner of the Brilliant BeDazzle Brewery and realtor in Brilliant.

"Did Miranda get ahold of you to ask about her house? Jezabelle yelled at Fleck from the kitchen.

"Yes, we are meeting for a meal tomorrow. We are going over to Fuchsia. We want to try out Rack's Restaurant. We can talk without being interrupted over there." He added as Jezabelle came out of the kitchen, "And I thought maybe she would see it more as a date."

Hick Rafferty picked that moment to enter the restaurant. He frowned, hearing Fleck's words. "Well, just don't cross her, or she'll kill you off in her next book. In fact, why don't you come here and I'll make sure she sees you in a different light."

Jezabelle rolled her eyes. "Fleck, I thought it was Lizzy you were interested in. Isn't Miranda a little young for you?"

Fleck laughed. "Haven't you heard of a May–December romance? Lizzy seems to have set her sights elsewhere."

"What about Phoebe? Not only is she rich and beautiful, but I've seen her flirting with you," Jezabelle reminded him.

The others were silently listening to the exchange until Hank spoke up. "I think Phoebe is taken."

"Taken?" The others all spoke at once.

"And you know this how, Hank Hardy? Is she taken by you?" Jezabelle's voice reached the shrill stage by the time she ended the sentence.

Hank stood up and indicated Hanna and Stick should join him. "I'm going home to catch a little shut-eye. Hanna, you and Stick go talk to the Pastor and his wife. Jeb is working on the break-in last night."

"I guess I better go to work too," Fleck said. He threw some money on the bar and proceeded to the door.

Hick yelled after him, "Remember, Miranda kills people."

Jezabelle turned to Hick after the others had left. "And what was that. Am I sensing you were warning him off?"

Hick's face turned a fuchsia shade of pink. "He's too old for her and he's a lothario. He's good at real estate and running the Brilliant BeDazzle Brewery and… truth be told, he's a nice guy, but he is a ladies' man and she deserves better than that. That's my opinion only." He turned and skipped into the kitchen. Sticking his face through the pass-through window from the kitchen to the dining and bar area he added, "We better get cracking; we'll be busy soon, and we close early today for Christmas practice. Remember? Did you ask Hank?"

Jezabelle wrinkled up her brow. "You know I should do that right now. Can you handle it for a little while? I will just toddle down to the police station and ask him."

"Um… Jezabelle, he said he was going home to sleep."

A sly smile crossed Jezabelle's face. "He did, didn't he. Well, I guess I will have to leave a message with Sadie. Maybe I can play blocks while I'm there."

She laughed as she went out the door.

Chapter Thirteen

"Hi, Sadie." Jezabelle greeted the woman sitting at the front desk of the Brilliant Police Station as she hurried by on her way to the back room.

Sadie stood up and moved quickly to stop Jezabelle. "Just hold your horses. You can't go back there. Besides, Police Chief Hardy isn't here; he's home resting after all the hoopla."

Jezabelle sidestepped Sadie. "I am not here to see Hank. I don't know why all of you think that I always want to talk to Hank. And... if you value your Christmas program, you will let me by because I need to talk to Jeb about playing... ah... ah... getting the donkeys inside the church."

"Donkeys? We aren't having live animals inside the church. That's not in my script."

"It is now. I thought it would add authenticity to the drama, and Pastor Sifter agreed and Nellie backed him up, and you know Nellie is really the one that rules what happens in the church except for the sermons."

Sadie thought for a moment and then moved out of the way. "Well, you can go on back, but be careful. There's a lot of glass back there. He is examining the blocks and pieces from the window. It's evidence you know, although I don't know in what because I am sure it was just some kids horsing around."

53

"You really have a thing for horses today, don't you?" Jezabelle commented. "Hold your horses, horsing around. It'll fit right in with the donkey." Laughing, she called down the hallway as she proceeded to the back room. "Jeb, maybe a horse broke your window."

Jeb came out of the back room. "Jezabelle, what can I do to help you?"

Jezabelle moved past him into the room and stopped at the large table where broken glass and stacked glass blocks lined the table. "I, ah… wanted to talk to you about a donkey in the Christmas pageant."

Jeb joined her by the table and laughed. "No you don't. Hank warned me you would be snooping but"—he shook his head—"nothing to see here. No fingerprints on the glass blocks or anything to indicate this has anything to do with Elfy's murder." He picked up a glass block. "We thought because of the way the window was broken there might be more to it than just vandals. They crushed the top blocks and then piece by piece took down the right side and the bottom row. Since we don't have an officer patrolling after two a.m. here, on call only, we think that is when it happened."

Jezabelle walked around the table, peering at all the blocks. "Did any one of the blocks have anything etched on it?"

"No. As you can see, they are all clear."

"Are you sure you have all of them?"

"As far as we know."

Jezabelle looked up as Sadie came into the room.

"I knew it. No donkey, right? Just Ms. Snoopy here?" Sadie remarked.

"No, there will be a donkey. We just got off the subject," Jezabelle answered.

"It's amazing the vandalism wasn't in this morning's Brilliant Times Chronicle. Snoop hasn't even been around pestering us for a story." Sadie turned and walked back to her office.

Jezabelle nodded. "That is strange, but then Snoop is always around when you don't want him around and never to be found when you need him."

"That's a good thing in this instance. We don't want the citizens of Brilliant getting all bent out of shape. Elfy's murder might have had something to do with his womanizing ways," Jeb speculated.

"His womanizing ways? I thought you didn't know anything about him."

"We haven't been able to find out who he is or where he is from, but he certainly didn't waste any time with the ladies of Brilliant. Do you know he even was romancing both Phoebe's mother and her sister, and neither knew about the other? I don't think Phoebe has heard yet." Jeb chuckled.

"Isn't that classified police business, and now you are spilling secrets?"

"No. We visited the BeDazzle Brewery and talked to Fleck and his staff. Apparently, that was Ernest's dating place of choice, but where they went from there we still haven't figured out. And it was whispered at the stable too while people were meandering around the manger scene. That guy that plays the shepherd heard it and so did Joseph and Mary. The only one it's been a secret from is Phoebe and apparently you. You just haven't been in the know—you and the Penderghast."

"The Penderghast Puzzle Protectors are no more. Hank forbade it. But if you would like to join, we have a new group, the Discombobulated Decipherers."

Jeb frowned. "What the heck is that and what does it mean?"

Jezabelle chuckled on her way out of the back room. "We don't know yet. We are deciphering it."

"Have you asked Hank yet?" Sadie yelled to Jezabelle's back as she rushed past Sadie and exited the building.

Chapter Fourteen

The church was buzzing with conversation when Lizzy, Hick, and Jezabelle entered.

"Wow, it looks like everyone made it for practice," Lizzy commented.

"Spread the word with our members that the Discombobulated Decipherers are having a meeting after practice," Jezabelle informed Lizzy. "Apprise Phoebe that we are meeting at her house. She doesn't know it yet. Tell her to make sure she has some wine. She is going to need it. I'll bring cheesecake."

Hick listened to their conversation. "Can I join?"

Jezabelle gave him a keen look. "You just want to join so you can see Miranda. We don't take slackers."

"I promise I have a good ear. And you would be amazed at what I know," Hick added.

"Okay, youngster, what do you know?" Jezabelle challenged.

"I'll let you know when I figure it out." He walked away into the crowd.

Phoebe and Mr. Warbler joined Lizzy and Jezabelle. "Did I hear my name mentioned?" Phoebe asked.

"Yes, we are having a meeting at your house. Are you stocked up on wine?" Jezabelle answered.

"My house—party at my house—when?" Phoebe asked.

"Tonight after rehearsal, I have news." Jezabelle's gaze scoured the room. "Look, even Santa is here, but I feel bad because we can't have Santa in a religious Christmas pageant."

"He could take off his Santa suit, and we could find room for him. After all, he is only here over the holiday season, and it would be nice to make him feel welcome," Mr. Warbler suggested.

"Maybe Sadie can ask him. Here she comes now." Lizzy moved aside to make room for Sadie.

"Where is he? Where is he? Didn't you ask him? We can't start without him." Sadie poked her face directly into Jezabelle's.

Jezabelle put out a hand and moved Sadie back away from her. "Calm down, girl. I didn't ask him, and no one else asked him either because we knew what the answer would be, so I have a plan."

"Well, that plan better happen fast because the practice is ready to start in ten minutes and you notice Hank is the only one not here. You would think he would have volunteered knowing the whole town is almost all here, and this pageant is famous all over our part of Minnesota. But no... he has a phobia for pageants because he is so afraid someone is going to ask him to speak. And he speaks well; he just doesn't know it."

Jezabelle broke in to stop Sadie's anxious rambling. "Now we all know he has a reason for that, and it goes back to when we were both teenagers at Brilliant High School and he had the lead in the Peculiar Perpetrators, and he got so into his lines that he fell off the stage, and after that he wouldn't even recite a prayer out loud or go up onto a stage."

"And you think he's going to do it now?" Lizzy asked.

"It's time for this sixty-year-old to find his voice and face his fear because he is good. Have you ever heard him sing?" Jezabelle asked.

"He can sing?" Warbler quizzed. "How do you know that?"

"I just do. Remember, high school. I have a long memory." Jezabelle tapped her fingers to her forehead.

"Well, just get him here," Sadie ordered.

Jezabelle picked up her cell phone. She tapped a key. "Hank, you have to get over to the church right away. We have a hostage situation. I can't see if they have a gun. No sirens. Jeb, Stick, and Hanna are already here, but their hands are tied. Quick, I have to hang up; they might hear me," Jezabelle whispered her last words.

"And what are you going to tell him when he gets here. And Hanna, Stick, and Jeb's hands are tied?" Phoebe worried.

"Look, they are tied. Jeb has the rope to the donkey tied around his hand so the donkey behaves while Mary is sitting on him. Hanna has the rope around her hand so the children holding on to it know where to go when they are led into the church. And Stick has hold of the rope on the handle of his walking stick, and it is wound around his hand." Jezabelle's face lit up with a smug smile. "Sadie, it's time to get everyone into place so we are ready when Hank gets here. Tell them to freeze and not move as if they are worried about something. This will work. It will."

"We forgot to ask Santa if he wanted to take off his suit and join the pageant," Warbler reminded them.

"You do it, Warby," Lizzy prodded. "Maybe a man-to-Santa talk would work." She shoved him in Santa's direction.

"Hurry, Hank has arrived." Jezabelle scurried to the front of the church and stood behind the podium.

Hank was in the narthex. Jezabelle could see him from her perch in the front of the church. He was being careful so no one saw him peeking through the glass in the closed door to the narthex.

Jezabelle began gesturing with her hands that Hank should quietly come to the front of the church as she pointed to the back of the altar.

Hank quietly made his way to the front of the church, checking to see each person in the aisle was safe as he quietly continued on down front, gun ready in case he needed it. He reached Jezabelle and said, "Who is the hostage? Where are they?"

"Put that gun away, Hank Hardy, the hostage is you. You are a hostage to your fears of speaking and singing ever since you were a teenager. We have decided it's time you took a leap of faith. You are the most courageous man we know in everything except this. We need you to be the narrator, and the narrator is a singing narrator. Here's the script. You haven't had time to practice, but it's fine if you make a mistake or two. You are among friends." Jezabelle stuck the script into his hands.

Hank stared at the script he held. He started to say something when a loud noise caught his attention. He looked up to see the entire cast peppered around the church standing and applauding.

"They are applauding for you, Hank Hardy. They know you can do this. What do you say?" Jezabelle said quietly.

Tears uncharacteristically welled up in the police chief's eyes. He cleared his throat. He opened his mouth to speak, but no words came out. He cleared his throat again and looked out into the crowd of onlookers. Nodding his head, he moved to the lectern.

"The stars were bright in Bethlehem that night so long ago."

Chapter Fifteen

Jezabelle's hair became damp from the snow falling as if a saltshaker was peppering her hair with white salt as she left the church. Hank touched her shoulder, stopping her from proceeding down the church steps.

"Thank you, Jezzy. I guess it was about time I got over my fear, although I could have throttled you when you put me on the spot like that," Hank acknowledged.

"Oh Hank, you were wonderful. We all knew you were right for the part."

"That we did, old boy." Mr. Warbler broke in as he passed them to descend the steps.

"Hank, would you like to come over for a nightcap?" Phoebe batted her long eyelashes and winked as she issued the invitation."

"Come on, Phoebe." Miranda grabbed her arm. "Remember we have plans."

"Sorry, Hank, you will have to be in Phoebe's clutches another night," Lizzy joked, grabbing Phoebe's other arm.

"What the...," they heard Warbler yell.

People on the steps let out a gasp. Someone yelled, "Is there a doctor still here?"

Hank hurried down the steps moving those in front of him out of his way. Jezabelle, Lizzy, Phoebe, and Miranda followed.

"Warby, are you all right?" Lizzy cried as she saw Mr. Warbler splayed out on the cement at the bottom of the steps.

"He's fine, a little shaken," Santa answered as he knelt by Mr. Warbler.

Dr. Winkler had followed the group down the steps having heard the call for a doctor and knelt beside Mr. Warbler and Santa. "Don't move, let me check you out. We may need to call the ambulance. Can you tell us what happened? Did you slip?"

Mr. Warbler pushed the doctor's hands away as he was attempting to examine him. "I'm fine and no I didn't slip. The step collapsed." He pointed to an area of the steps that was broken, leaving a gaping precipice at the bottom of the staircase. "I rolled—that's the upside to having such a rotund figure. It protects you when you take a tumble. It's called rickety rolling."

They turned to look where he was pointing.

"It does appear the cement has given away." Hank moved to the bottom steps for a closer look.

"Sweetie, maybe you had better have the doctor take a look at you? You were the first one here, Santa. What did you see?" Lizzie did her own examination of Warbler with her eyes as she waited for Santa's answer.

Santa shook his head. "Nothing really. I left the church a few minutes before the rehearsal was over. I wanted to wait until the real thing to see the ending, didn't want to spoil the ending, so I was down here at the bottom of the steps, but I was looking at the twinkling lights in the square when I heard Mr. Warbler call out."

"Let me help you up, Mr. Warbler." Dr. Winkler held out a hand. Nothing appears to be broken, but you should still come to the hospital so we can check you out better."

"Yes, I think that is a good idea," Lizzie agreed, pulling on Mr. Warbler's arm to help the doctor get him up.

Mr. Warbler stood up and shook the snow off him. "No, I have plans, remember, Lizzy? I am not going to miss the meeting. I guess I need to think of losing weight if I can collapse steps." He patted his protruding belly.

Phoebe eyed the steps and gave Jezabelle a direct look. "I think we had better be going. It's getting late, and Jasperine needs to be let out."

"Yes, yes, I have baking to do tonight. We will catch you later, Hank."

"Come on, Warby, I'll tuck you in and make sure you are okay." Lizzy, still holding on to his arm, began to pull him across the street.

Miranda, silently taking in the scene, said, "I ah... have a murder to commit in my new book that I am writing, The Glass Shattered, so I guess I will go home and shatter some glass over my character."

Before any of them could get any farther, Hank Hardy's voice rang out. "Hold it! If Mr. Warbler goes home with you, Lizzie, isn't he going to miss his meeting?" Hank asked suspiciously, "You wouldn't be planning anything would you, such as interfering in my investigations?"

Silence greeted his question until Lizzy spoke up. "Well..." She hung her head so she didn't have to look Hank in the eye. "It's supposed to be a secret, but I guess we have to... ah... let our secret out of the bag." She nudged Warbler.

"Secret? Our secret?" Warbler asked, confusion in his voice.

"That we are a couple, Warby, and your meeting was a night meeting with me. So now you all know. We are meeting." Lizzy pulled Warbler's arm and proceeded across the street, disappearing into the darkness and snow.

"They are a couple, and they coupled right under my nose and I didn't notice?" Phoebe complained. "I have been flirting with Warbler all these months for nothing?"

Jezabelle, who had turned back to eye the broken steps said, "We'll go now and let you and Pastor Sifter take care of this. Here he is now. Pastor?" She acknowledged the man who had just joined them.

"My, my, what do we have here? Was anyone hurt? I am so sorry I wasn't here sooner. I was talking with Sigfried Shepherd about a personal matter of his." He eyed the steps.

Phoebe gave the reverend a sharp look. "Sigfried Shepherd? What did he want? How long has he been in this town?"

Pastor Sifter eyed the nervous woman. "Not long. He is a new parishioner. Do you know him? And the reason people talk to me is that I cannot divulge what they tell me."

Santa had been watching the entire exchange quietly. "Ho, ho, ho. I think it's time for me to depart and get some sleep. I have a feeling it's going to be pretty complicated finding gifts for this crew." He turned and walked toward the square.

Jezabelle frowned. "Where is he staying?"

Hank shook his head. "I have no idea, but that's a good question. I'll have to look into it. He probably has a room at the Brilliant Bed-and-Breakfast. I think I will just follow you all home to make sure you get home safely."

"You go ahead, Chief Hardy; I'll put some barriers around this step until I can call someone to fix them. We don't want anyone else hurt. Good night." Pastor Sifter turned and walked back up the steps into the church.

"Really, Hank, there is no need to follow us home. This is Brilliant and there is safety in groups. You didn't get much sleep last night, and you had an anxious rehearsal so we will be fine," Jezabelle said, thinking of the meeting of the Discombobulated Decipherers they were supposed to have at Phoebe's.

"No, it's no problem at all. I want to stop at Rock's house and see if he's back yet. I'll follow your cars."

Resigned that Hank was going to follow them home, Jezabelle, making sure they were out of Hank's hearing distance, said to the others as they walked to their cars, "Go home and then give it thirty minutes, and we will meet at Phoebe's. Make sure Hank's car is not at Rock's before you leave your houses. Got that?"

Chapter Sixteen

Jezabelle watched as Hank's car pulled out of Rock's driveway right after he drove in. Apparently, Rock wasn't home and neither was Hanna. Just as Hank's car reached the end of the driveway, she saw Hick Rafferty's car pull up in front of Phoebe's.

"Rats, he must be here for the meeting. We didn't warn him," Jezabelle said to Mrs. Mysterious who was sitting at her feet.

She watched as Hank stopped his car and rolled down his window to talk to Hick. The exchanged a few words, and then Hank drove on. She wondered what Hick had told Hank. Hopefully not the truth, or they would have some explaining to do.

Grabbing her cheesecake, she opened her front door. Mrs. Mysterious slid through the opening before Jezabelle could stop her. Max, Mr. Warbler's hound, was waiting on the porch. As she stepped outside onto her porch, she eyed Jasperine and Mr. Shifty at the bottom of the steps. "You all must have a meeting too."

"Woo hoo, Jezabelle, get over here," Phoebe yelled across the street while letting Hick into her house.

Mr. Warbler and Lizzy came across his lawn to join them.

"We saw Hank leave. I wonder what Hick told him." Lizzy echoed Jezabelle's thoughts.

Miranda joined them and answered, "Hick is here? When did he join our group?"

"I begged Jezabelle. How did you think you would keep this a secret from me when you are all whispering all the time at the bistro?" he answered, peering out from behind Phoebe in the doorway.

The group stepped in past Phoebe and Hick. Phoebe peeked out into the night and then closed the door.

Lizzy poured the wine and passed it around while Jezabelle cut up the Peanut Butter Cup Cheesecake.

Phoebe sat down. "Should we bring the meeting of the Discombobulated Decipherers to order? Why are we calling ourselves by that name anyway, Jezabelle?"

Jezabelle handed Phoebe a piece of cheesecake. "Discombobulated means confused, and we certainly are confused. Decipher means to decode or unscramble, and we do that with puzzles. We think we are chasing another puzzle from the Brilliant brothers, so it makes perfect sense. As to why we are here? You were the reason we needed to have this meeting, but now after Warbler's tumble, I think we have more to discuss."

Lizzy handed Phoebe her glass of wine and said, "Drink up."

"Am I dying?" Phoebe asked suspiciously.

"Yes, is she dying?" Miranda asked. "What does Phoebe have to do with our meeting tonight besides providing us with a place to meet and wine?"

Jezabelle sat down next to Phoebe and took her hand. "Phoebe dear, your mother, and your sister were dating Ernest the elf. It appears he was a womanizer."

Phoebe pulled her hand out of Jezabelle's and stood up. "My mother and my sister—dating Elfy? Are you sure? No, that can't be. My mother doesn't date and my sister? She doesn't date either, although I have tried and tried to spiff her up and give her tips so she could catch a good one... No, that can't be."

Hick cleared his throat. "Well... it is true."

"How do you know?" Miranda asked.

"I saw them one night when I was at the casino between Fuchsia and Allure," Hick answered.

"They were double-dating one man?" Phoebe screamed.

Hick shook his head. "No, I saw Elfy two different times, once with your mother and once with your sister."

"And you didn't tell me?" Phoebe advanced on Hick.

"I didn't think it was any of my business."

"This puts things in a new light," Warbler commented.

Phoebe turned to Warbler. "What does that mean?"

"It means Ernest is dead, and your mother and sister were both dating him but one didn't know about the other," Jezabelle explained.

"Yes, and that might be taken as a good motive for murder," Miranda concluded.

"You can't actually think that my meek mother and sister would murder Elfy? They don't take after me. They are shy. There isn't a murderous bone in their body," Phoebe countered.

"And there is in yours?" Lizzy asked.

"What? No!" Miranda screeched.

"Well, the police might think something different," Jezabelle informed Phoebe.

"You think I did it, and that's why we are meeting?" Phoebe asked.

"No, of course not," Hick answered. "We don't, do we?" He turned to the others.

"We don't, do we?" Warbler echoed Hick's words.

"Phoebe, we know you didn't kill anyone and neither did your sister and mother, but someone did. And you know the

Brilliant Police Department doesn't always agree with us. We just need to be watchful. Now on to other business," Jezabelle continued. "Those steps didn't look like they crushed all on their own. To me, they look like they had been smashed by something."

"Why would someone smash steps and with everyone in the church?" Lizzy asked.

"Wasn't that the side where you found the glass block, Phoebe?" Miranda pointed out the detail.

Phoebe nodded her head. "It was."

Jezabelle got up and paced the room. "What if the glass blocks are part of a Brilliant Brothers puzzle, and whoever stole the glass block from the bank window, because it wasn't at the police station when I checked while I was visiting, was looking for the one you found, Phoebe?"

"But how would they know the block was there?" Mr. Warbler questioned.

"Well..." Miranda joined the conversation. "Suppose whoever murdered Elfy is the one that broke the step in the first place, looking for the glass block. He got interrupted by Elfy, and that is why Elfy was murdered. The murderer got scared away. In the meantime, Phoebe found the glass block and removed it."

"The murderer and thief went back to look for it, but it wasn't there. He might have thought it got pushed farther under the step, hence smashing the steps." Jezabelle finished the theory.

"That's kind of crazy and farfetched, don't you think?" Mr. Warbler offered his opinion.

"Are you making fun of Miranda's ideas," Hick growled.

"Relax, Warby." Lizzy put a hand on his shoulder. "It's about as farfetched as the floor puzzle, and that almost got us killed. And remember, Miranda has experience with mystery."

"Why wouldn't we have heard anyone smashing the cement while we were practicing the pageant? Isn't that risky?" Phoebe asked.

"The entire police department and most of the community was in that church. And the music was loud. We wouldn't have heard what was happening outside because the vestibule and outside doors were closed," Hick reminded them.

"We can't let anyone know we have the glass blocks. Hopefully, the thief wasn't inside the bistro when we had the one on the table. If this is what we think it is, then we would be in danger if whoever is looking knew. We need to figure out the value of those glass blocks and what they mean. We at least know the name that was on the third one," Jezabelle stated.

"What if we are on the wrong track?" Warbler asked.

"Then we are and we still had a little fun," Jezabelle answered.

"Santa was the first one at Warby's side," Lizzy pointed out.

"He was outside the church," Miranda agreed.

"Warbler, did you ask him to take off his suit and join the pageant?" Jezabelle asked.

"I did, and he said everyone would be shocked if he took off his Santa suit and saw his birthday suit. I left it at that. I saw the wild look in his eyes as he said it and decided to leave well enough alone."

"Wild look?" Phoebe laughed. "What is a wild look?"

"Well, his eyes got wide and they glared, and then he focused them right on me as if casting a spell. It gave me the heebie-jeebies."

They all laughed at the look on his face.

"Oh, Warby, you have been spending too much time with your birds and not enough time watching horror shows. You wouldn't know the difference between a smirk or lurk." Lizzy hugged him.

"What's next, Jezabelle?" Miranda asked.

Jezabelle doled out orders. "Phoebe, you need to talk to your mother and your sister. Find out what they know about Ernest the elf. Miranda, please look around your basement to see if there are any more clues as to why the glass block was where you found it. Lizzy and I will talk to Snoop Steckle and find out if he knows anything more about Ernest or has seen anything suspicious. He is always lurking."

"Where has Snoop been? We haven't seen him since he took that snap of you and your deer being stuffed into your house and put it on the front page of the Brilliant Times Chronicle," Lizzy reminded them.

"We'll find him," Jezabelle answered. "We just need to make some news. He'll be popping out of the woodwork and peck for details."

Chapter Seventeen

Jezabelle was putting the final touches on the cheesecake of the day when she heard Karen Smedley call out to her from the front of the restaurant.

"Jezabelle, you are needed out front."

Hick, who was chopping some veggies for the salad of the day, turned around and peeked out the pass-through. He broke into a full-blown, hearty laugh.

Hearing Hick's laughter, Jezabelle hurried out front. "What the...?" One by one, people were carrying in some form of plant or Christmas flowers.

"Where do you want us to put these?" Heddy from Heddy's Hot House Florals asked.

"What are all these?" Jezabelle asked.

"We were told to deliver them here. Don't have a name but just have the cash and a note." Heddy handed her the note.

"Sweetie, Christmas cheer because you are such a dear. Flowers from the heart, we've only begun to chart, our lives together, come calm or stormy weather."

Hick came up behind Jezabelle and read the note. "It appears you are planning a life with your secret admirer and you didn't tell us? When's the wedding?"

Jezabelle tucked the note in her pocket. "It's just someone trying to rattle me. No wedding, no charting, but I guarantee there will be stormy weather and soon when I get my hands on them. Enough of this nonsense. What am I going to do with all these flowers and plants?"

"Didn't I hear that you had a niece in Fuchsia that used to own Ella's Enchanted Forest? Maybe we should take them there," Karen suggested.

"Great idea. I will give her a call." Jezabelle turned to all the people holding plants. "Just put them anywhere. Karen here will arrange them until I call Delight."

The door opened, and Miranda shuffled in, stomping the snow off her boots. "That was quite the storm we had last night after we left our get-together."

"It was a quick snowstorm," Tom Burnside agreed. He was silently sitting in a booth sipping his coffee, watching the drama over the plants taking place. "It's a good thing most people have the Intelligent Icycles on their house so it melts the snow off their roof."

Tom was the owner of the company Intelligent Icycles, which made a roof wrap that looked like icicles that dripped but thawed the roof and put the water in barrels that froze and were hauled to the outside of town to decorate the sides of the road until they melted.

"There's quite a commotion in the square trying to get it all cleaned off so Santa and the nativity scene can go on. The stable really took a hit with the blowing snow. They are shoveling it out as we speak," Miranda informed the listeners.

Lizzy, coming in from the back having come through the tunnel from her house, commented, "I am so glad we installed some heat and insulation in that tunnel. It saves my wearing a coat and going out into the cold. Our architect should be here soon to see if we can make changes to our basement. Did we start a new greenhouse business?" She began to examine the plants sitting around the room.

Hick laughed and flicked a dish towel at Jezabelle as he went back into the kitchen. "No, Jezabelle's secret admirer struck again?"

Lizzy looked concerned. "You do know who this is, right, Jezabelle; you aren't in danger, are you?"

A thin, middle-height man with salt-and-pepper hair, a long black coat with a few holes in the sleeves, wearing khaki's that had seen better days, with feet wearing scuffed loafers and no socks, entered the bistro and sat down at the bar, saving Jezabelle from answering.

"I was wondering if I could get a warm cup of coffee." He fiddled in his pocket and pulled out change, counting it out and laying it on the counter. "I hope that is enough money."

Jezabelle eyed him up and down before answering, "It is, but it's almost Christmas, so the coffee's on us today. In fact"—she looked up at the others sitting in the bistro—"Free coffee today for everyone."

Lizzy brought a cup and poured him some coffee. "I don't recognize you. You must be new to Brilliant."

The man nodded his head. "I'm just passing through. Thought I'd stop for some coffee, and I heard about your Christmas pageant and the town square when I was going through Allure, so I thought I would stop for a few days."

Glancing at his bare feet tucked into his shoes, Jezabelle remarked, "Mighty cold and snowy for you to be without socks. Where are you staying?"

"My socks got wet, so I took them off and they are drying out. I am staying in a heavenly place. It's warm and toasty."

Before Jezabelle could ask more questions, the door to the bistro opened and a young man, Jezabelle guessed to be about forty, walked in carrying a clipboard and a bag. She left the bar to walk over and meet him. Extending her hand, she greeted him. "You must be Jackson Ritter, the architect."

"I am, and you must be Jezabelle Jingle. That is an interesting name." His smile lit up the room, and his blue eyes met Jezabelle's dead-on.

"It is, but that's a story for another time." She gestured for Lizzy to join her. "And this is the other half owner, Lizzy Langer."

Lizzy blushed under his gaze. "And how were the roads coming from Allure?"

"They were a little glazed, but it was no problem since it quit snowing. That was quite a surprise snowfall," he answered.

"Come right this way. The door to the basement is over here. Would you like some coffee first?" Lizzy offered.

"Let's have coffee after I have looked at what it is you want to do, and then we can go over the plans," he suggested.

"I'll have it ready for you when you come back," Hick yelled after the trio as they descended the steps to the basement.

"Interesting," Jackson said as he entered the cellar. Glancing around the space, he silently took note of every nook and cranny, walking farther into the room to examine the walls and the ceiling. "Now, tell me what you want to do?"

"We want to turn this into our wine cellar," Jezabelle explained.

"As in storing wine?" Jackson continued his perusal while speaking.

"No." Lizzy spoke up. "We want to move our night wine bistro down here and keep the upstairs just a coffeehouse."

Jackson nodded. "I see." He shook his head. "I don't know. This is an old building. And you would have to have an outside exit."

Jezabelle pointed to the basement window. "We found the original plans. That window was a door, and there was an outside entrance. We thought it would be perfect. I can see it now, a little canopy over outside steps alongside the building."

Standing on his tiptoes to peek through the window, Jackson remarked, "You would have to dig up the sidewalk and get permits but…" He stroked his cheek. "I suppose it could be done. It looks like something's happening out there. There are all fire trucks going by and police cars. This basement must be pretty solid and soundproof if we can't hear any sirens."

Jezabelle grabbed Lizzy and pulled her toward the steps. "Look around, we are going to see what is going on."

Opening the door at the top of the steps, the blast of sirens going by the bistro echoed in their ears. "Oh my, Hick, what is happening?" Lizzy yelled so she could be heard above the screaming noise.

Hick was looking out the front window. The bistro had emptied out when the fire trucks whizzed by. That's what happened in a small town. Residents figured they knew whoever it was happening to and wanted to see if they could help or gawk.

"Not sure. Hank and Hanna are over in the square, and Miranda took off to investigate. An ambulance just pulled up along with the fire trucks."

Jezabelle grabbed her jacket from the kitchen. She tossed a spare jacket of hers across the room to Lizzy. "Put this on. We better see if Hank needs our help."

"I'll help from here," Hick said. "I don't want to be part of the fire the firemen will have to put out if you try to help too much."

Jezabelle tossed Hick a disgusted look as she held the door open for Lizzie. "You better watch it young man, or you will no longer be one of the discombobulated ones."

Lizzy stopped short when she got out into the street. "Jezabelle, there's no fire. It looks like they are taking apart the wooden stable."

"But why?" Jezabelle left Lizzy standing in the street.

Hank saw Jezabelle elbowing her way through the crowd. "Now would be a good time to offer free donuts again, Jezabelle."

Pushing Sigfried Shepherd out of the way, Jezabelle stopped by Hank but not before having to push Sigfried out of the way again so Lizzy could get through.

"What's going on, Hank?"

Hank pointed to the back of the stable. "The city crew shoveled the stable out, and they heard a tapping toward the back of the stable. Snoop Steckle is trapped back there."

"What? How did he get trapped, and what was he doing underneath the benches on the back wall?" Jezabelle peered through.

"A better question might be why he didn't freeze to death if he was trapped there for very long. We haven't seen him in a while." Miranda joined the group after trying to snap some pictures.

"You're snapping pictures in these dire circumstances?" Jezabelle asked.

"What's good for the goose is better for the gander," Miranda answered. "Tit for tat, you know… He's certainly caught us in some compromising conditions, and I think it's time for him to be on the front page of the Brilliant Times Chronicle."

"Is he all right?" Lizzy asked Hank.

"He appears to be. We were able to drill a hole in the box so we could talk to him and… it's well padded and insulated. The insulation was meant to keep things warm. But I don't think we have ever built a seat at the back of our stable like it before. And the seams are sealed, so how he got in there and why it is padded and insulated is a puzzle. No, I didn't just say that—a quandary. I have to find out who built that thing and for what purpose," Hank answered.

"And the ambulance?" Jezabelle asked.

"Just a precaution. He says he has a gash on the back of his head and its fine, but we want to make sure we have medical help ready in case that changes when he gets out and he is mobile. The firemen should have him sawed out of there in a few minutes. They have to be careful to not hurt him. He is wedged in there pretty tight." Hank turned back to watch the progress of the firemen.

"Do you think we should cancel the town square Christmas with Santa and the nativity scene?" Jezabelle asked Hank. "After all, so many things have happened that we don't want any children injured."

"I have thought about that. But it is only a few more days until Christmas, and nothing seems to have happened when the events are open. We will put more patrol out here, and I think the kids should be safe. If we get too many complaints from worried parents we'll reevaluate the situation."

Hank moved forward to meet the stretcher carrying Snoop Steckle. The firemen had extricated him and handed him over to the ambulance crew. Hanna was accompanying them.

"Snoop, are you okay? How did you get in there?" Hank asked the scoop snoop.

Snoop's eyes opened and fixated on Hank. "And you are?"

Hank took a step back and looked at Angela Brooks, one of the Brilliant paramedics.

She shrugged her shoulders. "He has a pretty big gash on his head, and he's dehydrated and confused. You'll have to wait to question him."

"The good thing," Hanna explained, "is that whoever built the box also put a little heater hose in it that blows warm air into the seat. That's what kept him from freezing like Ernest."

"We need to find out who built the stable this year," Jezabelle interjected.

"Already did. Don't you remember the firemen built it this year? It was their service project," Miranda answered.

Jeb Jardine joined the group. "But they didn't build the seat at the back of the stable, and they don't know who did. Who knows what would have happened to Steckle if we would have canceled the town square event today because of the snow. He would have been buried under there longer. He was wedged in there pretty tight."

"It looks like we better round up Mary and Joseph and their crew and find out if they know anything. Hanna, you and Jeb interview them. I'll go to the hospital and interview Snoop and— Jezabelle, I hear your oven calling," Hank said with a glint in his eye.

"HH, we are out of the detective business. We are in the puzzle business, and I don't see any puzzle pieces here, do you? Make sure you are on time for the Christmas pageant on Christmas Eve. It's only a couple of days away, and I don't want you chickening out or using all this detective stuff as an excuse for dropping out of your role."

"To be there or not to be there, that is the question," Hank answered.

"Hank Hardy, you are no Shakespeare, it's to be or not to be." Jezabelle took Miranda's and Lizzy's arms as she threw the words over her shoulder at the detective.

"Ah but Jezzy, parting is such sweet sorrow."

"To be, Shakespeare, to be—and that's not a question, it's an order or the sorrow will be all yours." Jezabelle turned and came back and tapped his chest as she said the words, made one final tap, and turned away, pulling Lizzy with her down the street.

Chapter Eighteen

"You really want to make this into your wine cave?" Mr. Warbler asked Jezabelle and Lizzy as he sat down on the folding chair Hick had brought to the basement of the bistro for the group to sit on.

"What are we doing down here anyway?" Phoebe asked.

"We are having a meeting of the Discombobulated Decipherers," Jezabelle explained.

"Why are we calling ourselves that again?" Mr. Warbler asked.

"Because... you are all discombobulated and confused, so it fits perfectly. And we are going to decipher what those cubes mean," Hick answered.

"Well, since you wanted to be a part of us, I guess you wanted to be confused too," Miranda said.

"Maybe they mean nothing," Lizzy pointed out.

"If they mean nothing, why would someone break the bank window and steal one?" Jezabelle countered.

"Look," Phoebe interjected, "the last puzzle had real clues and it had the floor, but we have no clues and nothing seems to be popping up to give us any information. Maybe we are wrong."

"It seems strange that all these years no one has ever unearthed any of this, and now within the past year we have found two puzzles," Mr. Warbler pondered.

"Yes, but we wouldn't have known about any of it if the troubled twosome hadn't come to town and been looking for answers. They brought the information from outside of Brilliant and put us onto the puzzle by stealing our floors," Jezabelle reminded the group.

Miranda got up and paced the room, lit by candlelight because the group hadn't wanted anyone to know they were in the basement of the bistro. "What if someone new has come to town and knows of another puzzle. Perhaps they are descendants of the Brilliant brothers and found some information to bring them back and put them on track."

"Always a mystery writer, aren't you, Miranda?" Hick looked at her with an admiring gaze.

"Let's think about these cubes for a few minutes." Jezabelle broke into the conversation. "Last time, the pieces of floor put together a puzzle, and since the Brilliant brothers were puzzle makers, are these cubes part of a puzzle? If so, where are the rest of the pieces for us to put together?"

"What if whoever broke the bank window has the rest of the pieces?" Phoebe added.

"And do they know or do they not know we have two pieces?" Mr. Warbler began pacing with Miranda.

"Is it a coincidence we found the cube at the same time as Ernest the elf was killed? He was new to town," Lizzy pointed out.

"That is true, but remember the others lived here five years before they revealed their true character." Miranda sat down next to Hick. "You've been awfully quiet, Hick."

"I'm new here, so I'm just sitting back and learning from a beautiful, mysterious woman."

"Are you talking about me, Hick?" Jezabelle laughed, seeing Hick turn a brilliant shade of red. She continued. "Let's talk about the murder. Who would want to murder Ernest?"

"Me!" Phoebe said in a loud voice. "He was taking advantage of my mother and sister."

"And did you?" Jezabelle asked.

"Well, of course not. We've already established that earlier, but maybe one of his other women didn't take kindly to his flirtatious ways."

"Speaking of flirtatious ways"—Lizzy looked keenly at Phoebe—"what was that all about with that Sigfried Shepherd, Phoebe? He's new to town too, but you seem to know him."

"And he seems to know you," Jezabelle teased. "Considering he tried to interrupt your flirting with Joseph the other day and he discombobulated your usually flirty demeanor."

"Is this meeting almost over, and why aren't you serving us any wine? Isn't this supposed to be your new wine cellar soon?" Phoebe changed the subject.

"What are you keeping from us, Phoebe?" Mr. Warbler joined the conversation. "I happened to see Sigfried Shepherd sitting in his car in front of your house the other day when I was going out to feed the birds and the squirrels. When he saw me he left. He isn't stalking you, is he?"

"If that's the case, you need to tell Hank," Jezabelle advised.

Phoebe hesitated before answering in a whisper, "No, he isn't stalking me. He's my ex-husband, or at least I thought he was."

"What do you mean thought he was?" Miranda asked.

Phoebe shifted in her chair. "It appears we aren't divorced."

"You're married?" Jezabelle asked.

"No… no… just on paper. I thought we were divorced. I got a huge settlement. He is one of those billionaires, so he was generous with his settlement, or at least I thought he was. I was given misinformation by my attorney and papers that were fabricated. The divorce never went through. He didn't want the divorce, and so he paid off everyone to make it look like we were divorced, put all this money into my account so I didn't get suspicious, and then bided his time."

"Bided his time?" Jezabelle raised her eyebrows.

"He never wanted the divorce, and he has never given up on the idea he is my soul mate and I will come back to him. I thought it was done. I haven't heard from him in years since I moved back to Brilliant, but according to him, he was just waiting for me to come to my senses."

"He waited all this time for you?" You've been back here for years," Mr. Warbler stated.

"Exactly. I thought things went a little too smoothly, especially with the divorce settlement, but then I also knew he had a little snitzy sniggle on the side."

"A snitzy sniggle? Ooh, that's a good one. I need to write that down. I might use it sometime in my writing." Miranda dug in her purse for a pen.

"What's a snitzy sniggle?" Lizzy asked, perplexed.

"It's another woman," Jezabelle proclaimed. "That's why you got a divorce?"

"Yes, and the fact he was so secretive about everything. He left me alone in our huge house for weeks at a time. I will admit he was always generous with money, but I wanted a family and he didn't. Then I found out about his other life and that was it. He tried to tell me she was his sister, but haven't we all heard that story before?"

"Ah... no," Warbler replied.

"Don't think so," Lizzy added.

"Maybe." Jezabelle nodded.

"Only in my books," Miranda stated.

"I am really sorry for your snitzy sniggle problem, Phoebe," Hick said. "We need to get back on track. Do we or do we not have a connection with the glass blocks to the murders?"

"Not." Mr. Warbler voted.

"Not yet," Jezabelle stated. "For once, let's take Hank Hardy's advice and leave the murder to him, and we'll decipher the puzzle."

"Really?" All spoke at the same time, skepticism in their voices.

"I like that idea. I don't want to end up in another grave, and working with you people makes living dangerous," Hick reminded them.

"The idea, my dear Hickory, is to let the police do some of our groundwork, and then if we find the puzzle pieces fit the crime, we will put it all together for them. If HH thinks we are letting the murders go and not being snoopy, it will free us up from the prying eyes of the police, and who knows where that freedom will take us," Jezabelle explained.

Miranda shook her head. "Subterfuge, it's perfect for an undercover investigation." She jotted something on paper.

"Where do we start?" Phoebe asked. "Do you want me to distract Hank? I can invite him over for late-night dinners to keep him out of the way of your investigation."

"We start by looking at Miranda's basement nativity scene where she found the glass block," Jezabelle stated.

"And I will interview Snoop Steckle in the hospital, one journalist to another. He has asked me out, so it won't seem strange if I visit him," Miranda informed the group.

"He asked you out?" Hick asked.

"Great idea," Warbler chirped. "What should I do?"

"He asked you out?" Hick asked again. "You didn't accept?"

"Why Hickory, is there a reason I shouldn't say yes? After all, we journalists should stick together."

"Warbler, why don't you hang out in the square visiting with the parents that take their kids to Santa and the nativity scene? I understand there are going to be carolers tomorrow along with the Brilliant High School band playing music. Lizzy, I, and Hick need to man the bistro as it will be a busy time." Jezabelle finished her instructions.

"No, no reason, Miranda." Hick broke into Jezabelle's instructions to answer Miranda. "If we are done here, maybe I should see you home since the streets might not be safe this time of night."

"She came through the tunnel from my house," Lizzy said. "We can walk home together. She'll be fine."

Jezabelle, seeing Hick's deflated face, said, "Good idea, Hick. Check out her house to make sure no one is hiding there. After all, we must remember there is a murderer on the loose."

Hick's face lit up as Jezabelle made the suggestion. "Right, right."

Miranda put a final few notes in her the notebook and stood up. "Well then, Hickory, let's go."

With a twinkle in her eye, Jezabelle turned to Warbler. "You and Lizzy can go back through the tunnel by yourselves. I have some work to do here."

Warbler stood up. "Yes, yes we can. Come on, Lizzy, it looks like Jezabelle has some unfinished business yet tonight."

"Are you sure, Jezabelle? This bistro is only a few steps from the square and all the hoopla. I am not sure we should leave you alone."

"I will be fine. And you can lock the tunnel door after you get home. It's almost two a.m. now, so I think I'll just start my baking for the morning. I can catch a few winks later. I'll let Hick and Miranda out the front. See you in the morning."

"What about me? You've all given me the heebie-jeebies talking about the murder, and now you are leaving me to go home alone?" Phoebe chided.

"We'll give you a ride," Hick offered. "I'll drop you off and check your house if you want and then do the same for Miranda."

"Well, you can just drop me off. Jasperine will alert me if anything is off in my house," Phoebe acknowledged.

Hick, Miranda, and Phoebe followed Jezabelle upstairs as Lizzy and Mr. Warbler exited through the tunnel door.

"Are you sure you will be okay?" Hick asked Jezabelle as he held the door for Miranda and Phoebe.

"Right as rain or should I say right as snow since it seems to be snowing out again."

Jezabelle shut the door behind them. They had left the bistro dark with only the clock glowing on the wall for some backlight. Jezabelle looked at the time—two fifteen a.m. She quickly patted her hair and moved to the kitchen. Opening the fridge, she grabbed a couple of pieces of raspberry cheesecake, taking them and setting them on the bar. Moving to the wine rack, she pulled down a bottle of Brilliant Bordello Wineries' finest merlot. Opening the bottle, she poured two glasses. Hearing a tap on the door, she quickly lit one of the candles on the bar and put it near the wineglasses and cheesecake, creating a romantic glow. She hurried over to the door and opened it.

"I thought they would never leave," the deep voice murmured as he planted a quick kiss on Jezabelle's cheek.

Chapter Nineteen

The first person in the door of the bistro the next morning was again the scruffy, skinny man with the tattered clothes.

Jezabelle put a cup of coffee down in front of him. "You're still in town. Did you decide to stay awhile?"

The man nodded. "Yes, I want to see the pageant. I have nowhere else I have to be." He counted out some coins and laid them on the bar.

Jezabelle pushed the coins back at him. "Since you are new to Brilliant, coffee is always on me. It's my Christmas gift to you. Let me get you a piece of strawberry supreme coffee cake. I just took it out of the oven. Again, it's my treat."

The man shook his head. "I can't ask you to do that."

"You didn't. I like to be festive at Christmas. Where are you staying? I don't think you told me the location last time you were in."

"With a friend. It is a heavenly, warm place." The man sipped his coffee and then held on to the cup, warming his hands.

The Christmas bells on the door jingled as Santa came in. Seeing Jezabelle and the man at the bar, he sidled up and placed his rotund body on the barstool next to the tattered-clothed man. "Ho, ho, ho. Don't think we've met, but you look very familiar. I must have delivered presents to your home when you were small."

The man stood up and quickly pulled a stocking cap out of his pocket and plunked in on his head, down low over his eyes. Not looking at Santa, he muttered in a soft voice, "No, no presents when I was younger. You forgot me or I was a bad little boy." With those words, he turned and quickly left the bistro.

Santa's eyes followed him. "I am sure those eyes look familiar."

"It's a cold one out there today, Santa." Jezabelle peered into Santa's eyes, looking for a glint of familiarity.

"That it is." He winked at her.

"So what do you look like without the Santa suit?" Jezabelle asked.

"Why, my dear woman, are you questioning my authenticity? There will be coal in your stocking." Trying to distract the conversation he said, "How about some french toast with whipped cream and strawberries on top?"

Jezabelle frowned. "I only serve that to my friends. It's an off-menu item. How did you know about that?"

Santa laughed. "Ho, ho, ho. I know everything. Remember, I'm Santa."

Mrs. Mysterious picked the moment to come in through the back along with Lizzie.

"Shh. I know she is not supposed to be here, but she was pawing at my door wanting a visit and I decided to bring her along. We will keep her downstairs so the customers don't see her, but I brought her up for a minute to say hi to her human mom."

Instead of going to Jezabelle, Mrs. Mysterious spied Santa, hopped up on the bar and into his lap, and began purring.

"She is a little standoffish. She acts like she knows you. Does she?" Jezabelle gave Santa a suspicious look.

"Oh, oh, here comes the mayor." Lizzy reached over the bar for Santa to hand her Mrs. Mysterious. "We better get downstairs. I'll be right back." Lizzy disappeared through the doorway.

Mayor Astendorf, you are just the person I wanted to see. I think we should change our pet laws and adopt a law like Fuchsia, allowing pets to be in our businesses." Jezabelle threw out the suggestion.

Mayor Fred Astendorf nodded at Santa before sitting down at the bar. "They can be in some businesses, just not where they serve food."

"What if I opened a cat café?' Jezabelle countered.

"A cat café? What's a cat café? A place where cats eat?" Fred Astendorf's face crinkling up gave a clue as to what he thought of the idea.

Santa stifled a laugh.

"Yes, it is getting popular in large cities. Why... Well, I can't think of the city now, but I will get more information about it. I am going to open a cat café in Brilliant," Jezabelle announced.

Hick walked through the front door just in time to hear the statement. "Well, meow to you too, Jezabelle. Are your claws out this morning?" He nodded to Santa and the mayor before proceeding to the kitchen where his laughter exploded for all to hear.

"Ho, ho, ho. I think it's time I got back to my reindeer and got to work bringing happiness to the children of Brilliant. Do you want me to take a count when I am interviewing children to the number of cats that might frequent this café to see if it is profitable?" Santa gave another "ho, ho, ho" and almost skipped out the door in glee.

"Does he remind you of someone?" Jezabelle asked the mayor.

The mayor thought for a minute. "Yah, he does—Santa."

Jezabelle tapped his shoulder and said, "I'll get you some coffee."

"I hear we have a homeless man in town," the mayor said to Jezabelle when she brought him his coffee.

"I guess so. You just missed him. Strange fellow, but he seems harmless."

"Do you know where he's staying? Hank Hardy and I have been talking, and we think he might know something about Ernest the elf's murder and Snoop Steckle being locked in that seat in the stable."

"I've asked. He just says his digs are heavenly. And I never see him around except in the early mornings, and that's only been twice that he's come in. Maybe now he will come in more since I've told him eats are free."

"Do you think that's wise?" the mayor asked.

"Maybe not, but he seems like a good soul. He's got kind eyes, and maybe he is just down on his luck. It's my Christmas giving to do this for him," Jezabelle explained.

"Well, keep an eye and ear out. Hank and the police department don't seem to be able to find where he is staying or where he disappears to each day."

Jezabelle could hear Hick and Lizzy talking in the kitchen. "I need to go check on things. Good to see you, Mayor, and you better look into licensing for cat cafés. Or... you could just change the code for animals in Brilliant so people could bring their pets in while they eat. There must be some way around the health department rules. Your choice, change in rules or cat café." Jezabelle's face puckered at the thought of the mayor contemplating her threat.

"How are things going for lunch?" Jezabelle asked when she joined Hick and Lizzy.

"We were just talking about Snoop Steckle. Miranda called and she is going to visit Snoop, but she wants you with her.

We will take care of the lunch crowd while you and Miranda interrogate Snoop," Lizzy suggested.

"He won't talk to me. I am always shutting his snooping down."

"He will if you tell him who your secret admirer is," Hick teased.

"Or tell him you have a scoop on a new cat café coming to town." Lizzy broke out into laughter. "That was quite the imaginative threat to get the mayor to change the rules."

"Threat? I think it's a great idea. We need to look for a building, Lizzy. We will have the bistro here upstairs, the wine café downstairs, and the cat café somewhere nearby." Jezabelle rubbed her hands together. "I am going to be an entrepreneur at my age. And you are going to join me in my adventures."

Hick and Lizzy shared a look.

"Well, for right now, go and see Snoop and see if he knows anything about what is going on here, and maybe he knows something about the glass blocks." Hick untied Jezabelle's apron and took her coat off the coatrack and handed it to her. "Get the scoop from Snoop."

Chapter Twenty

"We are here to see Snoop Steckle. Someone said he can have visitors," Miranda informed the young nurse at the nurses' station on Snoop's floor."

The nurse pointed across from the station. "He's right there. We wanted him close. Good luck. He doesn't remember much at all and has tried to do some wandering. We have to watch him like a hawk." When she realized what she said, she began stammering. "Ah, I am sorry. You didn't hear that, did you? I was um... talking about me. Privacy rules you know, and I am a little frustrated right now so I am confused too. Go right in."

The door to Snoop Steckle's hospital room opened, and Snoop proceeded across the hall to join them at the nurses' station. "Nursy, who brought these boring clothes for me to wear? I am going to be let out of this place soon, and I can't be seen on the street wearing these." He held up a pair of khaki pants and a tan shirt.

"Well, you wore them in here along with a sweater and jacket, but they were taken as evidence by the police and brought back. I guess those are the same boring clothes you wore before," The nurse answered. "And—I am not nursy. I am Nurse Ratchett."

Jezabelle and Miranda's eyes widened at the name Ratchett. Jezabelle said, "Did you say Nurse Ratched such as the nurse Ratched in the book *One Flew Over The Cuckoo's Nest?*"

The nurse skewered them with her eyes. "No. Rachett as with two *t*'s not a *d*." Nurse Rachett with two *t*'s turned to Snoop. "But believe you me, I can act like Nurse Ratched, so you better get back to your room. You aren't supposed to be wandering. Got that?"

Before Snoop could reply, Miranda took one of his arms and turned him back toward his room. Jezabelle grabbed the other arm before turning to Nurse Rachett. "We've got this."

"Come on, Snoop, let's get you back to your room." Miranda patted his arm.

"Do I know you? And I am not Snoop, I am Snodley."

"Snodley?" Jezabelle held back her laughter.

"Yes, Snodley Steckle, a journalist for the London Times."

"Snodley Steckle? London Times? Suppose you tell us all about it," Jezabelle said as she closed the door of his room.

"Who are you?"

"Snoop, it's us. You are always snooping on our lives. Don't you remember the reindeer and the picture you took of us trying to get it into my house because you are trying to find out about my secret admirer?" Jezabelle reminded him.

"Or when you took a picture of us pulling up Phoebe's floor, and Hank arrested us because he thought we were the floornappers?" Miranda added.

"Nope and nope," Snoop said, shaking his head.

"So, Snodley, how did you get trapped in the box in the stable?" Jezabelle asked, thinking she would jar his memory.

"Yes, that was unfortunate. I decided to visit this fine community to cover the Christmas pageant for the London Times. People in London are very interested in small-town America's Christmas tradition. I was taking a night shot with my camera, and my bulb rolled into the box, so I had to crawl in to get it out."

Jezabelle frowned. "But it was a sealed box, and last I heard they weren't sure how anyone could get in there. The rescuers were baffled, and they had a hard time getting you out. So how could you crawl in?"

"Who are you again?" Snodley asked.

"Snoop, it's us. Come on, we are here to help. How did you end up in the box with a gash on your head?"

"Nurse Ratched, help! They are trying to confuse me? Help!" Snoop screamed.

The door to Snoop's room flew open. "What is going on here, and I told you it is Rachett with two t's not a d. It's time for you to leave. You are upsetting my patient, and he is already a basket case."

Snoop frowned. "I am not a basket case, I am a box case. I was found in a box."

"Fine, we will leave"—Jezabelle turned as she reached the open door—"but we will be back."

Miranda followed Jezabelle out of the room. They stopped when they were out of hearing distance of Snoop's room.

"Do you buy that? He can't remember?" Jezabelle asked Miranda.

"Or Snodley and the London Times? Where did that come from?" Miranda shook her head.

"Either he has an active imagination or he is conning us, but why?" Jezabelle pointed down the hall. "Look, here comes Hanna. Let's ask her."

"Ladies, why are you here?" Hanna asked.

"Just checking on Snoop. Have you seen him yet?" Miranda questioned.

"Yes, that is why I am here. He doesn't remember anything. He seems to have come up with a different personality and different name—and a different newspaper he works for. I am here to get more information and to bring him new clothes so he can be discharged. He doesn't like the clothes that he was wearing when we found him." She held up a duffel bag.

"Yes, we heard that. Do you think it is for real?" Jezabelle asked.

Hanna shook her head. "The doctor says he took quite a hit on the head, so it could have triggered his amnesia and caused him to think he is someone else. I'm taking him home to see if that jars his memory."

"And if it doesn't?" Miranda wondered.

"Time will tell," Hanna answered.

"When is Rock coming back?" Jezabelle asked.

"Can't say," Hanna answered.

"If you don't know, who does?" Miranda asked. "He could be a big help to us?"

"Us who?" Hanna queried. "You are not supposed to be doing anything, remember?"

"We aren't," Jezabelle explained. "We just miss him, and we have a new puzzle we are putting together that has nothing to do with the murder. He's good at puzzles, but I guess this one we have to go alone."

"You do that, and I won't tell my father." Hanna held up the duffle bag. "I better get these to Snoop or should I say Snodley. Stay out of trouble." Hanna continued down the hall to Snoop's room.

"What do you make of that? They believe him?" Jezabelle said, pondering the dilemma.

"This is Snoop we are talking about. Could he be conning all of us because he knows something and wants to be the first to solve it or... because he knows something and he is scared of the consequences if he talks?" Miranda suggested.

"Could be either," Jezabelle agreed.

"I have to get back to the bistro because of the festivities in the square this evening. Let's meet at your house after we close the bistro, then examine your basement nativity scene. Why would they carve a nativity scene into your basement wall, and why would there be a piece that would come out? Is the rest of it glass?" Jezabelle asked.

Miranda shook her head. "No. You will see. I love my finished basement. It is unique. Broderick Brilliant did a wonderful job when he designed the house. And it is so different from the rest of yours. I'll contact the others."

Chapter Twenty-One

The sound of "Jingle Bells" being played by the Brilliant High School band in the town square could be heard in the Brilliant Bistro as Jezabelle and Lizzy mingled with their customers, serving them hot mulled wine and Tom and Jerry's.

Mr. Warbler stomped his feet to release the snow from his boots as he entered the bistro. He gestured to Jezabelle and Lizzy to join him at the big window facing the street. "You have to see this," he said with a huge smile on his face.

Jezabelle took one look out the window and burst into laughter.

"What is it? Lizzie elbowed her way in between Mr. Warbler and Jezabelle. "Well, I guess that explains the complaining about the clothes," Lizzy commented.

"So, this must be Snodley." Jezabelle could barely spit the words out as she was choking from laughter.

"Snodley? Who is Snodley? All I see is Snoop Steckle in his red glory. Do you suppose he thinks he is Santa Claus?" Warbler continued oogling out the window.

"That, my dear Warby, is the former Snoop Steckle who now thinks he is Snodley Steckle from the London Times. And his old clothes are too boring." Lizzy took his arm.

"I guess we can't call his attire boring now." Jezabelle was mesmerized by the bright red overcoat trimmed in black leather accompanied by a leather wide-brimmed hat matching the leather on his coat. Red leather boots completed the ensemble along with a polka dot red-and-fuchsia scarf.

"Do you want to explain all this to me?" Mr. Warbler asked.

"We are all meeting at Miranda's later. We will explain then. Did you see her at the festivities or Phoebe? They are wandering around there somewhere." Lizzy turned back to inspect the tables to see if any of their customers needed anything.

Hick seemed to have everything under control. Lizzy watched as he handed out free drink tickets for the Brilliant BeDazzle Brewery. Fleck Flaherty was giving out tickets for free Tom and Jerry's for the Brilliant Bistro at the brewery. The cross-promotion works well for both businesses. Though it may seem they did the same thing at night, the bistro was more laid-back, and the brewery had more custom drinks and high-end cuisine.

"I didn't see Miranda, but I did see Phoebe. Nellie Sifter talked her into joining the carolers. Actually, I think she just did it to avoid Sigfried Shepherd at the stable. He kept taking breaks as a shepherd and herding his sheep over by Phoebe as she was wandering around, so when Nellie asked her to join them, she didn't even hesitate," Mr. Warbler explained.

"Oh, the carolers are at the door and they are coming in to serenade us." Jezabelle moved to open the door let them in. "Hick, get some Tom and Jerry's ready for the carolers."

"Got it," Hick answered from behind the bar.

Thirty carolers entered the bistro causing a space problem, so Jezabelle invited them up to the front bar and indicated some should stand behind it to make more room while they sang.

"Oh goodness, thank you, thank you," Nellie chirped in her soft voice. "We are going to start with "Away in a Manger" and then we will go into "Oh, Holy Night" with a solo by our own Phoebe Harkins." Nellie turned and lifted her arms to direct.

"Phoebe can sing?" Jezabelle whispered to Hick as they made the Tom and Jerry's."

"I guess we will find out," he answered.

Lizzy and Mr. Warbler, standing by the door, felt a sweep of cold air as the door opened and Sigfried Shepherd entered the bistro.

"Mr. Shepherd, I think Mary and Joseph need you over at the stable," Lizzy suggested, stopping him from coming farther into the restaurant.

"Joseph sent me to get something warm for them to drink, and I see I am just in time for another concert from the carolers. I'll wait until they are done to get the drinks."

Warbler turned to Sigfried. "We know you are stalking her. Maybe Snoop did too and you decided to keep him away from Phoebe too. He was known to flirt with her once in a while."

"Warby, let's just go with the flow and listen." Lizzy grabbed his arm and dragged him across the room with her to the door by the kitchen.

The carolers finished "Away in A Manger" and began to sing "Oh, Holy Night." Phoebe stepped forward and began to sing a solo. The bistro became very quiet as the first notes came out of her mouth.

Jezabelle's mouth dropped open.

Hick stopped making the Tom and Jerry's.

Lizzy put a hand to her mouth and clutched Mr. Warbler's arm tightly.

Mr. Warbler's eyes teared up.

The notes coming out of Phoebe's mouth were breathtaking and beautiful, each note perfect and at times sensuous.

"And we didn't know," Jezabelle remarked.

"How did Nellie know?" Hick asked.

Lizzy tapped Jezabelle's arm. "Look, Sigfried Shepherd is moving toward Phoebe. We need to stop him. He'll ruin this beautiful moment for her."

Before they could do anything, Sigfried Shepherd started singing right along with Phoebe, and it became as if the two were one, harmonious in their art. The patrons of the bistro were mesmerized by the sound. Soon the rest of the carolers joined in as a backdrop to the two people who seemed oblivious to anyone else in the room.

When the song finished, the entire audience stood and clapped for the two performers.

Siegfried gazed into Phoebe's eyes before breaking the spell and turning to Jezabelle. "Could I have five hot chocolates to go, please?"

For a moment Jezabelle couldn't speak. "You just tipped us topsy-turvy with that surprise and then you ask for hot chocolate as if nothing happened."

"Nothing did happen. It was a professional performance. No more, no less," Phoebe piped in.

Noticing the friction starting to spark, Nellie Sifter spoke up. "We must move on carolers, back to the square and then on to the Brilliant Benevolence Home. Can we take the Tom and Jerry's you made with us? Her eyes transmitted a message to Jezabelle, indicating they needed to get Phoebe away before the melee started between her and Sigfried.

"Yes, yes—Hick, give them their Tom and Jerry's. Stay away from the police so we don't all get in trouble," Jezabelle warned.

"And don't give them to the old folks at the home," Warbler called out. "There's a full moon tonight, and you know what happens in the Benevolence Home on a full moon. Add the Tom and Jerry's and the nurses all will quit."

Hick looked at Warbler after the carolers filed out. "What happens at the Benevolence Home during a full moon?"

"There is a theory that a full moon brings out the mischief in older people with memory problems. Maybe they remember what they were doing by the light of the silvery moon when they were younger," Lizzy answered for Warbler.

Jezabelle gave a stern look to Sigfried Shepherd who came to join them while he was waiting for the hot chocolates to take back to Joseph and Mary. "Is there something you want to add? How long are you going to be in town? You seem to be upsetting Phoebe."

"Yes, and I see you stalking her outside her home," Warbler added. "I won't stand for it."

Sigfried turned to Warbler. "And what will you do?"

"Is that a threat?" Lizzy asked.

Sigfried shook his head. "I just need to explain to her how I feel and why I let her think we were divorced, but she won't give me the time of day, so all I can do is stalk her."

"Well, perhaps you should rethink that. She doesn't want anything to do with you," Hick interjected.

"There is so much you don't know. But you will. And Warbler, I see you coming back and forth during the night between your house and Lizzy's house." Siegfried again addressed Mr. Warbler.

"Is that again a threat?" Warbler's voice raised and squeaked.

"And... that is old news. For your information, his studio is behind my house, and even if it was me he was coming to see, what business is it of yours?" Lizzy chided.

"It isn't any of my business; I'm sorry I didn't mean to antagonize you, I just wanted hot chocolate and to try to get you to plead my case so I can talk to Phoebe and explain." Sigfried picked up the tray of hot chocolate that Hick had set on the counter. "Good day."

The group watched him leave. Hick looked over the other patrons to make sure they had what they needed, then said,

"Maybe he has something to do with the murders. He is new in town. He is in the stable. He is stalking Phoebe, and maybe he didn't like that Phoebe met Ernest the elf."

"This is getting complicated," Lizzy said.

"It is. First, we have Snodley who is really Snoop, who has completely changed personalities and doesn't remember how he got in that box. Phoebe has a Siegfried stalking her, and they used to be married, but wow, can they sing together. And... we have the possibility of another puzzle. Are they connected? Jezabelle said, listing the unusual details.

"We can discuss this all at Miranda's later. But where is Miranda?" Lizzy asked.

"Hick, it appears to be thinning out. Lizzy and I will go and look for Miranda. She should be in the square. Want to come along, Warbler?" Jezabelle got her coat off the hook in the kitchen.

"No, I'll stay here. I really like this mulled wine. I think I'll have some more and stay warm. We'll see you at Miranda's when the festivities are over."

Lizzy eyed Warbler. "Hick, make sure he doesn't overdo the mulled wine or he might get lost traipsing in the snow between his studio and my house if he decides to go there after our nighttime meeting. Or he might decide he wants to do a little mulling with Phoebe's mom when she is sitting for her painting at two a.m. And Phoebe has enough to worry about without her mother and Warbler getting wined together."

Hick frowned. "Phoebe's mother sits for you at two a.m.? What do you do? Why do you have a studio?"

Warbler's eyes shot daggers at Lizzy. The only people who knew about his shadowy work were the Penderghast Puzzle Protectors group, and Hick hadn't been a part of that.

"It's okay, Warby. He is now part of us. Remember the Discombobulated Decipherers. He can know," Lizzy soothed.

"I can know what?" Hick asked.

"We'll fill you in later unless Warbler wants to fill you in while he is mulling his wine," Jezabelle answered. "We need to see what's happening at the festivities. Come on, Lizzy. Let's be festive."

Chapter Twenty-Two

"Aren't all the lights pretty tonight?" Lizzy twirled around, taking in the scene on all sides of the square.

"And the Intelligent Icicles add to the décor. If you look down the streets at all the neighbors who bought the icicles to keep the snow off, all the roofs are twinkling, making the entire community look like a winter wonderland," Jezabelle agreed.

"There is quite a crowd tonight. Santa looks busy. His new elf seems to be working out well."

"Do you see Miranda anywhere?" Jezabelle asked.

"There she is on the sleigh ride. And she is holding on tightly to Fleck Flaherty. He's driving and she looks like the snow queen next to him. Hick isn't going to like that."

"Miranda doesn't have a clue that Hick is interested. And I have to think she is cozying up to Fleck for some reason other than trying to not fall off the sleigh when the horses dressed like reindeer come to a sudden stop."

"What should we do now?" Lizzy asked. "Everything looks normal here."

"Let's mingle at the manger scene and see if we can work our way to behind Mary and Joseph and take a look at that box that Snoop got caught in," Jezabelle suggested.

"Won't we be noticed?"

"Well, I need a place to plop and enjoy the festivities and it looks like that box behind them is the only place there is to sit. After all, I have worked all day you know." Jezabelle inched through the crowd of people and made her way to the stable.

Sigfried Shepherd nodded as Jezabelle walked past him and asked, "Something you need?"

"We need to sit a spell. I understand tomorrow the baby is going to join you in the stable." Jezabelle sat down behind Sigfried and his sheep. She didn't know what happened to Lizzy.

Mary turned around to Jezabelle and said, "Yes, and I am excited. Abraham Miners is going to be our baby this year, and he is adorable. I hope we can keep him warm. Apparently, that is why they built the seat behind us so that we could open it up and put him in it to keep him warm."

"But… it doesn't open. The firemen had to cut Snoop out as he was stuck. They didn't know how he got in there," Jezabelle reminded the woman. "Why they put it back together and sealed it again though is strange."

Joseph turned around. "I can't believe you don't know that they solved that mystery."

Jezabelle raised her eyebrows. "They did?"

"Yes, the church boiler room is underneath the box. There is an opening to the basement of the church. It is a room and hallway separate from the main basement of the church and is underground. No one knows why, but the custodian who built the box decided to build it over the trap door that they found underneath a bush that had been here. They dug the bush up in the fall and found the trap door," Joseph explained.

"And no one told us?" Jezabelle asked.

"They didn't tell anyone. They were afraid someone would try to break through and get into the church. They decided to leave it there because if they needed to put in a new boiler or furnace, they could lower it down that way. It's probably why the trap door was there in the first place." Joseph expanded on the explanation.

"So why couldn't they get Snoop out?" Jezabelle asked.

"You'll have to ask Hank," Mary answered. "Rumor is that the custodian wasn't around and neither was Pastor Sifter and... no one else knew about it, and since Snoop happened to be filling the space, they couldn't find that out."

"Apparently, Snoop found it and that is how he got in. But that doesn't explain why you think it was built to keep the baby warm." Jezabelle challenged the answer.

Sigfried Shepherd sighed and joined the conversation. "Because the custodian hadn't decided the design and cut the doors for the baby. He was trying to decide whether they should look like barn doors or just a door that we could remove so we could watch the baby while it was in there."

"What? What? That makes no sense. It's a little late to try to cut in the doors if the baby is going to be here tomorrow night. Who told you that tale?" Jezabelle asked. "I again don't understand why they put the box back together and didn't put in the doors for the baby."

All three answered at once, "Hank Hardy, Chief of Police."

Jezabelle gave all three a skeptical look. "I guess I will have to talk to Chief Hardy. Have you seen Lizzy? She was right behind me."

Jezabelle felt a tap underneath her on the bench. She looked around. No one else paid notice. Maybe she was imagining it after the tale she had just heard. Another tap startled her bottom. She looked down. Soon she saw a finger come out of the hole the firemen had cut out to talk to Snoop that had still been left on the side of the bench. The finger tapped her leg.

Jezabelle looked around, making sure no one was watching her. Mary and Joseph and Sigfried were busy talking to some children who came to see Mary and Joseph and pet the sheep. The sheep hid Jezabelle from their view.

She leaned down by the finger and heard Lizzy whisper. "Come into the basement of the church. I'll meet you there."

Jezabelle inched her way around the edge of the crowd, silently sneaking away so Mary and Joseph and Sigfried didn't notice. She would go in the back door of the church if it was open so no one saw her.

Taking a glance at Pastor Sifter and Nellie's house, connected by a walk at the back of the church, she saw that the house was dark. Looking around, she saw Nellie arriving with the carolers back from the Benevolence Home. It was dark behind the church, so even if Pastor Sifter was home, he wouldn't see her. What were the chances the door was unlocked?

She snuck into the dark shadows and tried the door. It was open. Stepping into the small foyer, she got out her cell phone to light her way. She noticed the lights were on in the sanctuary. She smacked her forehead with her hand. Why hadn't she checked to see if the lights were on in the church? Someone was up there. Lizzy must have snuck past them, or maybe she came in a back way too.

Listening, Jezabelle heard a melody of one of the songs in the Christmas pageant. The voice was deep and vibrant. Hank was practicing! For a moment she stood and listened and then moved to the steps to the basement. Using her flashlight to guide her, she took her time so she didn't find herself tripping and rolling to the basement.

"Jezabelle, is that you?" Lizzy whispered.

"Yes, where are you?" Jezabelle peered into the darkness before turning her light in the way of the voice.

A light came on illuminating Lizzy's face. "Over here. I found the boiler room. Did you know it existed and it was under the ground over by the nativity?"

"I just found out. Phoebe's Sigfried told me. It's kind of creepy down here without any lights."

"I heard them tell you, so I snuck away to investigate. How did Sigfried know?" Lizzy asked as she took Jezabelle's hand to lead her back into the boiler room.

"According to him, Hank Hardy told them. I can't believe Hank didn't tell us."

"Probably because he didn't want the Discombobulated Decipherers to get involved," Lizzy answered.

"Look, there is a trap door underneath the bench." Lizzy turned on a small light in the boiler room. There were no outside windows to give their snooping away.

"But how did Snoop get trapped?" Jezabelle whispered as she moved the door up and down.

"Maybe someone stuffed him in there and latched the door holding him up in the box. It is pretty tight in there," Lizzy suggested.

"I guess that makes sense. It is really sturdy when you latch it. According to Joseph aka Herb Lynch, there was supposed to be doors built from the outside into the box so they could lay the baby in there to keep warm. That is why there's a heated hose blowing in from the heater."

"Why weren't the doors built?"

"Apparently, our illustrious custodian couldn't decide on the design."

"Well, where is George? We will have to ask him." Lizzy latched the bottom of the box and turned her cell phone light back on while turning the boiler room light off.

"I haven't been looking for him, but now I think we need to flush him out. We have to be quiet. Hank is up in the church practicing, and he is the last person we want to catch us here."

They quietly made their way up the steps to the back door of the church. Hank's voice could still be heard filling the sanctuary with music. As Jezabelle opened the back door, it hit something solid.

"Ow, you could be careful with that door."

"Snoop Steckle, what are you doing here? Jezabelle asked as she and Lizzy stepped outside.

"It's Snodley. I don't know who this Snoop character is. And what you are doing here—in the dark, I may add."

"Why, um... we were here listening to Hank practice. He's shy and wouldn't let us watch him, so we decided to stand by the bottom of the steps and listen," Jezabelle answered.

"Oh, that chief of police. Yes, I recognize that name. He asked me questions. He too thought I was this Snoop Steckle person."

"Did you ever remember who hit you on the head and stuffed you into that box?" Jezabelle questioned.

"My dear woman, no one stuffed me anywhere. I hit my head when I got off my flight from London at the Minneapolis-St. Paul airport on my way here for a story. When I got to Brilliant, I must have passed out and they put me in your hospital, and then all of you came to me with that crazy story. I have to be somewhere. Good night." Snoop tipped his hat at them and walked away.

"Do you think this is an act, or that knock on the head really knocked him into making up that imaginary person?" Lizzy commented.

"Or was he following and spying on us when we went downstairs to the basement in the church? But then... he didn't try to hide when we came out. It looks like things are winding down in the square. Let's go back to the bistro and help them close and then get to Miranda's."

"Yes, I want to know why Miranda wasn't Ice Queen up there with Fleck Flaherty." Lizzy giggled

"Don't you mean Snow Queen?"

"No. Ice Queen because she usually freezes him out unless she needs information for her books. And he is such a nice guy although a little bit of the ladies' man, that he keeps trying to thaw her out."

"Well, maybe she melted."

Chapter Twenty-Three

That was quite the crowd tonight." Warbler moaned as he plopped down on Miranda's sofa.

"You just aren't used to serving hot chocolate and wine at the same time, Warbler." Hick heckled him.

"I'm not used to it at all. Give me my birds and squirrels any day. They chatter and I pretend to know what they are saying. It's different with customers; I have to remember their order. Never do that to me again, Jezabelle—leave me alone with your patrons." Mr. Warbler wiped his brow.

"And me." Hick laughed. "I thought he would start tweeting at them—and not the internet kind of tweet. Let's all tweet like the birdies tweet."

"It's comfy in the basement too. Come on down and let's get sleuthing," Miranda invited.

"We've already been sleuthing," Jezabelle informed the group.

"Without me?" Phoebe complained.

"You were singing with the choir and trying to avoid Sigfried," Lizzy reminded her.

"Wow, this is beautiful, Miranda," Phoebe remarked, touching the beautiful stone walls that were finished with a white shimmery coating.

111

A fireplace stood at one end of the large family room in the basement. The pattern of the stone on the fireplace was different than the walls; each stone had an inspirational word carved into its middle section. The floors were two different types of brick, laid out in a walkway, meandering through the basement and into the other rooms. The ceiling was finished with white tin tile, which had flower indentations in the middle of each tile.

"And it is dry down here, not moldy or musty. How did you pull that off?" Mr. Warbler asked.

"I have a dehumidifier in the summer, but I have had no moisture. They must have done something to the outside to seal it. After all, they weren't the Brilliant brothers for nothing. And none of the residents touched this or changed anything, it appears. It is amazing all our houses survived the wear and tear of people who didn't know their history. Come over here." Miranda walked down one of the hallways.

When the group followed her, they found the carved nativity scene in the wall of the hallway.

"This is where I found my glass block. See here is the indentation where it sat." She pointed to the square, empty two-by-two hole.

Jezabelle studied the scene. "Was our glass block the only thing that was loose in this carving?" She pulled and poked at the Wise Men carved on the wall.

"It is. The block was a gift one of the wise men held in his hand. See—the gifts of the other Wise Men are carved but not loose, and each shepherd has something different, but not a block of glass. The gifts are frankincense and myrrh. That is why I poked at the glass block and found it came out. It didn't fit with frankincense and myrrh. But then I thought perhaps they were going to put the names on the Wise Men and instead changed to the gift names." Miranda stepped back away from the wall to let the others get a closer look.

"This is a puzzle," Phoebe remarked before moving back to the family room in the basement and sitting down on the sofa.

The others followed, each finding a cozy place to sit.

"Did I tell you I am adopting a dog and a cat?" Miranda informed her friends.

"Wonderful. Mrs. Mysterious and Mr. Shifty could use another cat in the neighborhood to hunt with since Max and Jasperine don't always understand that there are some places dogs just can't go," Jezabelle commented.

"So spill. What did you mean when you said you were sleuthing?" Phoebe asked.

"Have you talked to Sigfried lately?" Jezabelle threw out the question to Phoebe.

"Not if I can help it," Phoebe quipped. "I'm working on actually getting that divorce out of him, and I cannot be responsible for what I say to him, so I thought it was better to avoid him."

"Well, you should cozy up to him a little and get some information. He seems to know what is going on in Brilliant. He and Mary and Joseph told me the story of the seat in the manger. Apparently, George, the custodian, built it to keep the baby warm. It sits right over the trap door to the boiler room of the church." Jezabelle rubbed her hands together, getting into the story.

"Trap door to the boiler room?" Mr. Warbler chirped.

"Yes, a trap door that was under a bush they removed, and they found the door, so they decided to leave it. And then they gave us a cockamamie story about George not getting an outside door for the baby built because he couldn't decide what kind of door," Lizzy piped in.

"And the door still isn't built, and the baby is due tomorrow in the manger scene, and for some reason the firemen put the bench back together just like it was after getting Snoop out," Jezabelle finished.

"Maybe George will put the door in tonight," Phoebe mused.

"And Hank knew about all this. He kept it from us," Jezabelle stated.

"And then when we were sneaking out of the basement, Snodley was sitting on the steps and caught us." Lizzy jumped up. "I think he was following us."

"Snodley?" Warbler's face betrayed his confusion. "Oh, that's right. Snoop who thinks he is Snodley."

Miranda, standing by the fireplace, moved over to a desk in the corner. "He is Snodley. He really is Snodley." She threw printed copies of articles from the London Times from ten years past.

Snoop Steckle's face stared up at them from the front page of the paper.

Phoebe picked up the paper and said, "He's an award-winning journalist."

Mr. Warbler looked over her shoulder. "Well, it sure looks like him."

"He's been here about eight years under the name of Snoop Steckle," Miranda said as she picked up the paper. I have contacts in London, and I have emailed them to find out more about this. From what I can find, Snodley just quit the paper one day and disappeared. He left a note saying he was leaving London and they shouldn't try and find him."

"So that hit on the head made him forget he was pretending to be Snoop and he became Snodley? Don't you think the paper would have checked his credentials, and why would a world-renowned journalist end up in Brilliant?" Lizzy asked.

"We will see what my friend says," Miranda answered.

"We are getting off track, although the answers to our puzzle might lie with Snoop and who put him in the box and why." Jezabelle began following the bricks that made a path in the basement.

"It would be nice if Rock were here to help us out. He has the connections and the sneakiness to help us with this," Phoebe reminded the group.

Jezabelle nodded. "Every time I ask Hanna about him she just says he is out of town. He sneaks in and out, and I never see him at his house. She is very evasive."

Hick had been quietly observing and listening to the conversation. "As I see it, we need to talk to George and we need to latch on to Snoop and find out if this is a ruse. And—we need to find that third block. You have the other two safely hidden here, right Miranda?"

"Why, Hickory, you have picked up on the deciphering of sleuthing very well. I think we can now consider you a full-fledged member," Jezabelle teased.

"You have been awfully quiet tonight. Were you upset you had to work when the rest of us were having fun?" Miranda taunted.

Hick stared at Miranda for a moment and then answered, "Not all of us can parade around in a sleigh and pretend to be a queen for the night. What were you doing, research for your next mystery? I can see it now: Snow Queen flecks off flares of flirting."

Miranda ignored him and turned to Jezabelle. "I think I should have a go at Snoop or Snodley. He has asked me out before. Maybe I can get him to talk."

"You tried that once in the hospital," Hick reminded her.

"We had too many people around to work my mysterious ways with him."

Jezabelle coughed to hide her laugh. "I think that's a good idea. You are assigned to Snoop."

"I'll see if I can find George and talk to him," Warbler volunteered. "I have some questions about building a bird sanctuary in my yard, and I know he has some experience in that field. I will have him show me the box and chat it up with him."

"I thought we were solving a puzzle, not a murder?" Hick reminded them.

"Isn't it all the better if we solve both? Hank needs our help. He just doesn't know it. He has all he can do to learn his part for the Christmas pageant." Jezabelle walked back down the hallway to the nativity scene on Miranda's wall. "This is beautiful. But it is a puzzle. I know it is. There are three blocks. One was found here. One was found at the church, and the other was found at the bank. Why are they scattered all over town, and why did someone steal one? Hick, we need you to mind the bistro tomorrow afternoon. Lizzy and I are going for a walk around town to see if we can spot any other puzzle pieces."

"I will continue my research on Snoop and see if I can find out anything more about the Brilliant brothers after they left Brilliant. I've tried before and it has been sketchy, but I have another idea," Miranda commented, seeing them to the front door.

The street was quiet as they left Miranda's house. Only the moon and the twinkling icicles on the houses shimmered in the night.

"Isn't that Sigfried Shepherd's car parked in front of your house?" Warbler asked Phoebe.

"Is he dangerous?" Jezabelle stared at the car trying to see if Sigfried was sitting in it waiting for Phoebe.

"No, he is just annoying," Phoebe answered as they walked to their end of the street.

"Do you want me to call the police?" Miranda, standing in her doorway, yelled down the street after them.

"No, I will take care of it."

Lizzy walked back across the street from her house to join Warbler, Jezabelle, and Phoebe. "Well, since you have to see him anyway, pump him about the seat in the manger. He may know more than he is letting on."

"I guess now is as good a time as any to see what I can find out and maybe get him to sign those divorce papers." Phoebe left the group to go over to the car in front of her house, turning back to warn them. "And once you get home, I expect to see your curtains all the way down and not a movement from your houses. I can take care of myself."

Jezabelle watched her proceed to Siegfried's car. "She's been awfully serious lately. Not her usual flirty, silly self. Give her time to get in the house, and if he goes with her, all eyes on deck."

Chapter Twenty-Four

It's a beautiful winter day for a walk, don't you think Lizzy?" Jezabelle remarked as they left the Brilliant Bistro.

"I guess. I am still tired from staying up so late last night plotting with the Discombobulated Decipherers. Oh, I love that name." Lizzy laughed. "It fits us perfectly. We are such a crew of bumblers, but don't tell anyone I said that."

"Our bumbling hides our true intellect," Jezabelle reminded her.

"Where are we walking?"

"I think we need to observe the street. The steps of the church are cleaned off. Let's sit a minute. After all, that is also where Phoebe found her glass block, underneath the crumbled steps."

They walked down the street to the steps of the church.

"The steps aren't fixed yet," Lizzy pointed out.

"It's hard to pour concrete in the winter." Jezabelle peered into the barricades cordoning off the crumbled part of the steps.

Lizzy climbed the steps and sat down midway between the street and the entrance to the church. "I think it can be done under certain conditions. Somewhere I read that you can use warm water, and the concrete must be kept in a warm area prior to mixing. Then they use warm blankets to cover it, and then they must use a waterproofing concrete sealer. And it must not be introduced to snow or water within seven days of the project. You can also throw straw over it to insulate it."

Jezabelle joined her on the steps. "Really, and since when did you become a concrete genius?"

"I don't know if what I am telling you is exact. Before I came back to Brilliant, I dated a concrete guy. We broke up because I told him he was made of stone just like his concrete. He never smiled." Lizzy laughed and made a stone face.

"We surmised that the glass block Phoebe found when she kicked the steps were hidden there for a long time. What if we change our thought process on that? What if there was the tiny hole in the cement and whoever had the glass block hid it there recently for some odd reason?"

"Who? It had to be someone who knows there is a puzzle. Do you suppose the other residents of Brilliant are looking for puzzles now that we made them aware that there are puzzles to be solved?"

Jezabelle stood up on the step.

"Be careful," Lizzy warned. "We don't want you taking a tumble."

"It was the same night Ernest became a twinkling statue. Maybe whoever took care of Ernest hid it in the steps first. Maybe they were trying to keep it from Ernest," Jezabelle surmised.

"Or maybe Ernest had it, hid it in the steps before he became the victim."

"But if that's the case, then who broke the window at the bank to get the block? And who has it now? Wouldn't they have taken the block hidden in the steps if they knew about it?"

"Ladies." Snoop Steckle stood at the bottom of the steps looking up at them. He proceeded up the step and sat down next to Lizzy.

"Snoop, is there something you need?" Lizzy scooted over while Jezabelle sat back down.

"Snodley, not Snoop. Don't you remember anything?" Snoop fidgeted, rearranging his long coat over his knees.

"I think it's you who isn't remembering who you are, Snoop," Jezabelle reminded him.

"Since when did you start wearing dressy wool overcoats?" Lizzy fingered the material.

"My dear woman, this is the correct way for a reporter from the London Times to dress, and its Snodley."

"Well, Snodley, why are you here sitting next to us on the steps?" Jezabelle asked

"Why are you sitting on the steps in the cold?" Snodley countered.

"Have you seen Miranda today, Snodley? I think she was looking for you." Lizzy changed the conversation.

"Yes, I am meeting with her at the Brilliant Brewery. It's confusing all these Brilliant names in this community. That would never happen in London, trimillion duplicate names. I fancy her, and so I was very excited when she asked me to communicate with her at the brewery. I want to also do a story on her exciting career as a mystery author, as long as she doesn't kill me off to further her book."

"Trimillion? I don't think that's a word," Jezabelle pointed out.

"When I speak, the dictionary listens. It will be soon. Since you are not privy to any earth-shattering information for the London Times, I will leave you here to ponder the steps or whatever it is you two are pondering. Good Day."

Snoop/Snodley tipped the top hat he was wearing on his head and moved down the steps and along the street away from them.

Jezabelle shook her head. "That top hat makes me think of the *Cat in the Hat*, but I didn't want to laugh."

"What do you think? Is he faking it? I couldn't tell," Lizzy asked.

"I think he is. I think he was trying to see what we know. Maybe he's afraid of whoever stuffed him in the box."

"Where do we go from here? This didn't accomplish much except for my fingers to turn blue from the cold." Lizzy clapped her hands to warm them up.

"Look, isn't that the homeless man that keeps coming into the bistro in the mornings?" Jezabelle turned Lizzy in the direction of the town square.

Lizzy's eyes narrowed as she tried to pick the man out of the crowd. "I wonder where he is going. He seems to be in a hurry."

"And look. Santa just put down the child on his lap and quickly followed him."

Lizzy started down the steps.

"Wait for me," Jezabelle said as she followed Lizzy. "Let's follow him too."

The two women got to the bottom of the steps and looked toward the back of the square.

"Where did they go? They aren't at the nativity scene. Did they go to the back of the church to the parsonage? Why would the homeless man go to the parsonage? There's nothing else back there." Jezabelle indicated to Lizzy with her hand that they should take the sidewalk alongside the church to the back.

When they reached the area between the church and the parsonage, it was empty.

"Maybe they are visiting Pastor Sifter and Nellie. Maybe they are helping the homeless man. Isn't that what pastors are supposed to do?"

"Let's look in the church." Jezabelle held the heavy back door open for Lizzy.

Lizzy stepped into the small vestibule. "Which direction—up or down?"

"Up."

They climbed the steps and opened the door to the sanctuary. A surprised Santa stared at them from the opposite wall of the church where a big red heart was carved into the wall.

"Oh, we're sorry; we didn't know you were in here." Jezabelle faked her surprise at seeing Santa.

"No, no problem, ladies." Santa moved through the pews to meet them. I... ah... was just getting warm. Needed a little break from the little ones, you know. I always feel bad when I can't grant their Christmas wishes, but when they ask for a trip to Madagascar because of the movie, I hate to disappoint them, but I know I would be on the parents' blacklist if I granted that wish."

Jezabelle frowned. "I am sure I know you from somewhere. Fess up, who are you under that beard and suit?"

Santa ignored the question and instead asked, "How is your stuffed reindeer? Rudolph was impressed that you have a replica of him in your home."

"You know about the reindeer?" Lizzy asked and then looked at Jezabelle. "He knows about your reindeer. Is he your secret admirer that you won't tell us about?"

"What? NO! Don't you think I would recognize it if it were H... ah... George," Jezabelle answered.

"George? George as in the custodian here?" Lizzy blurted out.

Jezabelle put a sly smile on her face. "Maybe." She then turned to Santa. "Are you stalking me?"

"No, Santa does not stalk anyone, but I am Santa, so I know all. Excuse me, ladies, I hear the children calling."

He walked through the door but not before Jezabelle caught a whiff of his cologne.

"I know that cologne, but I can't think who wears it," she said and quickly went to the top of the steps to yell after Santa, "Did you see the homeless man come in here?"

"Homeless man? I haven't met a homeless man, but let me know if you find him, maybe I can leave him some presents on Christmas to help him out. Ho, ho, ho."

Jezabelle turned back into the church to join Lizzy. Lizzy was staring at the wall next to them toward the front of the church.

"You know, I always took this nativity scene carved into this wall of the church for granted. Do you suppose it has something to do with our puzzle?"

Jezabelle ran her hands over the carving of the nativity scene as it was large and started from the floor and went halfway up to the ceiling and took up half the side of the church. "Maybe. We will have to take a better look at this later with the Discombobulated Decipherers. There is our rehearsal tonight before the pageant. Perhaps we can all sneak back in after the church is closed. We do our best work at night."

Lizzy looked around the darkened church. "Where do you suppose the homeless man went? Perchance he really did go to Pastor Sifters and Nellie's. But it looked as if we startled Santa when we came in."

"We've got to get back. We both need to do some baking, and that architect fellow is coming back late afternoon to give us the news on whether we can do something with our basement. I forgot to tell you," Jezabelle apologized.

"One more thing." Lizzy lowered her eyes. "Do you suppose you could invite your secret admirer to dinner and I could have you and whoever and Warby over on New Year's Eve?"

"As in a date? At your house? A New Year's Eve date?"

"Yes, and I could meet your secret admirer. After all, I am your best friend. It'd be fun. You don't think Warby is dating Phoebe's mother, do you?"

Jezabelle held the door of the church open and indicated Lizzy should precede her down the steps. Remembering Warbler's visit earlier in the week asking about Lizzy, Jezabelle answered mischievously, "Well, maybe."

Lizzy turned around at the bottom of the steps and looked up at Jezabelle, giving her a flabbergasted look before flouncing out the door.

Jezabelle laughed. "Something I said?"

Chapter Twenty-Five

The bistro was full of people when Jezabelle and Lizzy got back. Hick yelled from the kitchen, "Finally. That was a long walk. I need some help here.

"I'm working as fast as I can." Karen Smedley yelled over the crowd as she waited on a table in the corner. Addressing Jezabelle and Lizzy she warned, "He's a little crabby this afternoon. Watch out."

"What's got your knickers in a knot?" Jezabelle asked Hick when she joined him in the kitchen while Lizzy helped out in the dining room.

"I don't like our plan." Hick huffed out the words.

"What plan?" Jezabelle answered, looking closely at Hick and noticing his pouty look.

"The plan where Miranda meets Snoop or Snodley or whatever his name is. You know he's been a crass flirt since he came to this town."

Jezabelle laughed. "Patience, boy, patience. I think Miranda can handle herself."

"That's not all," Hick complained.

"All what?"

"She's then going to Fuchsia with Fleck Flaherty for a late-night dinner at Rack's Restaurant after pageant rehearsal

125

tonight." Hick slammed the oven door as he put a pan of Jezabelle's famous rum coconut bars in the oven.

"Careful. We don't want the bars to flatten from your door-slamming technique," Jezabelle warned. "She is just searching for information or trying to make you jealous."

Hick stopped what he was doing and turned to Jezabelle. "She might be trying to make me jealous?"

"I didn't say that." Jezabelle smiled. "Jackson Ritter is here to tell us if we can remodel the basement. Ponder that thought." She tapped the counter beside Hick before motioning to Jackson to follow her down to the basement.

"Hick looks a little bewildered," Jackson said as they reached the bottom of the steps.

"He's young. You remember what that was like, right?" Jezabelle asked the handsome middle-aged man.

"It must be a woman. Maybe I should give him some advice about women." Jackson laughed before rolling out the floor plan onto a shelf. "We should be able to do what you need down here. It's going to take some work. I talked to city hall, and they will let you dig up the street and put the door back in. You need to talk to Rachel Robin, the city administrator, about the permits. She can be a little persnickety, so I would do it soon if you want to get started on this by spring."

Jezabelle looked at the plans. "I will show these to Lizzy and see what she thinks. I don't know why she didn't follow us down here."

"I must be moving on. Give me a call when you are ready to proceed. I have to get over to the church. Pastor Sifter wants to talk about building a bell tower onto the church that can actually have a working church bell."

"That is strange, isn't it? Although it has been a long time since anyone has questioned why the Brilliant brothers built and enclosed the bell tower without any way up there and no bell." Jezabelle shook her head. "They were unusual people."

"Rumor has it that the church was being built when one of Broderick Brilliant's daughters died. The child loved church bells, and they were going to put a beautiful bell up there. The child died in the middle of the construction, and when it came to the tower, they were in so much grief that they ordered it to be a solid tower with no way up and closed forever because they felt their hearts would be closed forever because of their loss."

"And then they abandoned the town, and no one that moved here in the early days seemed to care that the bells were missing?" Jezabelle asked.

"According to Pastor Sifter's wife, Nellie, who apparently researched this, the residents decided to leave it that way after they heard the rumor, to honor the Brilliant brothers wishes. But now Pastor Sifter and the church council think it is time to add on a new tower with a church bell, but they are leaving the old tower in honor of the founders."

"Wait a minute. How did the Sifters find all this information, and why haven't I heard the rumor?" Jezabelle asked suspiciously.

Jackson shook his head. "I don't know. I just found out too. You will have to ask the Sifters. I have to get going. Have a merry Christmas." He turned and walked up the steps.

Jezabelle followed him up the stairs. When she reached the top of the stairs, she couldn't believe what she saw. All the animals from the Penderghast neighborhood were in the bistro, mingling with the customers.

"What are they doing here?" Jezabelle asked Lizzy while trying to catch Mrs. Mysterious.

"I did it." Mr. Warbler was standing by Jeb Jardine, who was having coffee with Sadie Noir. Warbler was holding Mr. Shifty while his dog Max sat by Jeb, waiting to be petted.

"You can't have them in here. We will get shut down." Jezabelle's alarmed expression matched her voice.

"It's a test," Mr. Warbler answered. "You want to start a cat café, and I thought we could add dogs, so I brought them down here to see how they would react and what the customers would do."

"And they love it, both the furry creatures and the humans." Lizzy patted Warbler on his shoulder. "Good idea, Warby."

"I have another reason for popping in. George the custodian has disappeared. He is nowhere to be found."

A pot banged in the kitchen. Then they heard the oven door slam.

"What's wrong with him?" Lizzy asked.

"It's a Miranda thing," Jezabelle answered.

"He has a thing for Miranda?" Mr. Warbler asked.

"You might say that, and right now she is at the Brilliant BeDazzle Brewery having an early cocktail with Snoop," Jezabelle explained.

"Snodley," Lizzy corrected her.

"And later," Jezabelle continued, "she is going to Fuchsia and Rack's Restaurant for a late dinner with Fleck, after the pageant rehearsal."

"Whoops. The mayor is coming across the street, and it looks like this is his destination. We need to hide the critters." Lizzy grabbed Max's collar. "Warby, grab Jasperine. We'll hide them in the basement until he leaves."

Jezabelle watched as they hustled the animals down the basement steps, and then she turned to her customers. "The critters were just a figment of your imagination. If you keep quiet while the mayor is here, I'll give you a free piece of the cheesecake of the day. Hickory, I am joining the others in the basement. Make sure the mayor gets free cheesecake too." She turned and hustled down the basement steps before the mayor entered the restaurant.

"I just heard some news that may or may not be true," Jezabelle informed the other two when she joined them. "Jackson Ritter is at the church, looking into building another bell tower."

"Two bell towers on one church? Doesn't that seem excessive?" Lizzy asked.

"It would be nice to have a bell tower with a bell. I've always wondered why we have a bell tower that is just a closed-in cement tower with no way up there," Warbler added.

"According to Jackson, the rumor is one of Broderick Brilliant's children died during the building of the tower and this child loved the bells. They were so grief stricken that they closed up the tower so no one could ever access it again," Jezabelle explained.

"Another mystery for another day," Lizzy commented. "How did Jackson know this?"

"The Sifters."

"Miranda has been doing research and she didn't uncover that. So how did they?" Lizzy pondered.

"That's for them to know and us to find out," Jezabelle stated.

"Do you suppose it has anything to do with our mystery?" Mr. Warbler asked.

"Or Elfy's murder?" Lizzy added.

"I really do feel discombobulated now." Lizzy frowned.

"The pieces aren't adding up," Warbler agreed.

"That's because we haven't deciphered them yet and we don't have many clues except the glass blocks. We must be missing something." Jezabelle walked over and pulled Max away from trying to dig underneath at the wall beneath the window. "Control your dog, Warbler. He's trying to dig out my door in the wall too early."

"I'll take the critters back home and come back for practice at seven. I'll use the tunnel to your house, Lizzy, and get my car tonight." Warbler gave a whistle.

The dogs ran to Warbler's side. The cats just looked at him.

Lizzy laughed. Jezabelle reached down and scooped up both Mrs. Mysterious and Mr. Shifty and put them in Warbler's arms.

"I don't think your whistle works for these two, Warby." Lizzy gave him a peck on the cheek.

Warbler almost dropped the cats before turning and disappearing through the door to the tunnel.

"Now Lizzy, you shouldn't lead the poor man on," Jezabelle warned.

"He has no idea where I am leading him," Lizzy answered with a huge grin on her face.

Chapter Twenty-Six

J ezabelle, it's good you're here." Pastor Sifter met Jezabelle at the door of the church.

"And why is that?" Jezabelle asked as she glanced over the hubbub of people waiting for pageant practice to start.

"This small package was left on my desk with a note to deliver it to you tonight." He handed her a small square box wrapped in white paper with a small heart-shaped bow on the top.

Miranda, Mr. Warbler, Lizzy, and Phoebe, who arrived with Jezabelle, leaned over her shoulder to see what she had.

"Open it, open it!" Phoebe chanted.

"I'll open it later. It's time for rehearsal."

"I'll leave you to your decision," Pastor Sifter said, turning away to talk to another parishioner.

"Wait." Jezabelle grabbed his arm. "Jackson Ritter told me you are thinking of building a new bell tower and that you have information on the Brilliant brothers."

"Yes, it seems there is a story to the tower after all. It was strange, but Nellie found a couple of pages of a book stuffed in a crevice underneath the baptismal font. It couldn't have been there very long because we move the baptismal font to the middle aisle when we have a baptism. Otherwise, it sits and fits right in the grooves on the floor. It is quite a unique design

131

as you well know. The stone font turns and unlocks from the base on the floor. A few days ago, she found the pages that explained why we have the unusable bell tower. They were very old pages. It's another mystery for you to solve, but in the meantime, I decided it is the time we let go of the past and start a new chapter with a new bell. I must go and get ready for rehearsal."

"That's interesting," Phoebe said, "but I am more interested in your gift. Is it another gift from your secret admirer?"

"Yes, Jezabelle, we are all friends here and we saw the other gifts. Are you sure someone isn't stalking you?" Lizzy asked.

"I'll open it just to satisfy your curiosity," Jezabelle answered, irritated by their questions.

She slit the tape fastening the top to the bottom of the box. She lifted the cover and peeled back the tissue paper to reveal two rings looking to be from the sixties. Immediately tears formed in her eyes.

"It's an engagement and a wedding ring? Are you getting married? Do you know what they mean?" Phoebe peered closer into the box.

Jezabelle picked up the rings and stared at them. "I do." She thrust the box at Lizzy. "I have to leave for a few moments." Jezabelle turned and moved through the back doors of the narthex, disappearing from their sight.

"Oh my." Lizzy looked at the rings.

"She's upset." Warbler looked toward the back of the church. "Should we go after her?"

"No, she's back." Phoebe pointed down the aisle.

"It's time to get the show on the road," Jezabelle said with Hanna by her side. Hank followed them. Jezabelle's demeanor was back to normal.

"Are you sure you are fine?" Lizzy whispered in her ear as they went to take their place in the pageant.

"Yes, I just needed a few minutes in the ladies' room, but I ran into Hanna and Hank before I made it there." She leaned across Lizzy to give instructions to the rest of the Discombobulated Decipherers. "Not a word of what was in the package I received—understand? To anyone. You didn't see it. Phoebe, do you understand?" Jezabelle raised her voice when talking to Phoebe, then grabbing the box out of Lizzy's hands, she stuffed it in the pocket of her dress.

"Fine, just fine, but you don't say a word to me anymore about Sigfried and we've got a deal. Hush. We are starting." Phoebe put a finger to her lips.

Nellie was making an announcement. "I understand this is a very religious time, but I want this pageant to include everyone and I had a request. After conferring with my husband, I made a decision. Santa would like to be a part of this pageant. As you know, according to Santa, he can't take off his suit because he's the real deal." Nellie rolled her eyes indicating her disbelief. "So Santa would like to kneel at the manger of baby Jesus and make a statement about Jesus being the real reason for Christmas, not Santa, and I decided to honor his request. That's all, folks. Let's get started."

The room erupted in conversation.

"What do you think of that?" Lizzy asked, perplexed.

"I think Santa looks familiar, but I can't quite place him." Jezabelle stared at the man in the red suit. "And why not include Santa especially if he honors the real reason for Christmas."

"And then there is Snoop or Snodley." Lizzy pointed to the man dressed in a suit covered with red poinsettias.

"What did you find out, Miranda, when you had drinks with him?" Jezabelle asked.

"I'll tell you later—the practice is beginning."

"Since you have a late-night rendezvous with Fleck, why don't we meet at your house early in the morning, Lizzy? Say five a.m. Since we closed the bistro for practice tonight, I'll just stop by and put a sign on the door that says we are going to be closed until ten a.m. to get ready for our Christmas open house tomorrow night," Jezabelle informed the group.

"What Christmas open house?" Hick had just arrived and sat down next to Miranda.

"The one we are going to have tomorrow night that no one knows we are having." Jezabelle laughed. "But it's a good excuse to be closed."

"We can have a wine-and-dine special and announce your plans to open the basement as a wine cave," Hick suggested.

"And Miranda can perform," Lizzy added.

"What? No I can't perform. I don't perform. I write books."

A booming voice came over the microphone. "If those loud party people in the back of the church would pipe down, we can get on with practice." Hank looked directly at Jezabelle.

Jezabelle glowered at Hank and lowered her head.

Hank began reciting his lines.

Jezabelle looked off to her right in the direction of the large heart carving on the wall of the church opposite of where they were standing. She nudged Lizzy, turning to her to whisper, "Look, it's the homeless man. He's by the heart. This is the first time I have seen him taking part in anything."

Lizzy lifted her head and looked in the direction of the heart. "I don't see him."

Jezabelle turned back in the direction of the heart. He was gone. Her eyes scanned the room. She couldn't see him anywhere.

"Maybe it was someone that looked like him?" Lizzy suggested.

"No, it was him. He sure disappeared in a hurry."

"I hate to interrupt your interruptions of our hearing when it is time for us to participate, but I think it is time for us to participate." Phoebe stood up and pulled Lizzy with her.

They said their lines together as Mary rode the live donkey to the front of the church. They followed Mary and Joseph.

Hank began to sing "O Holy Night."

Tears welled up in Jezabelle's eyes as she listened to his rich voice sing the beautiful words. Soon Sigfried Shepherd joined in the song. Jezabelle took a sneak peek at Phoebe's face. Her face looked like it was a carved stone statue.

The thought made Jezabelle glance across to the side of the church where she had seen the homeless man. Something glinted on the floor next to the heart. She looked around. No one else seemed to be looking in that direction, and everyone in the pageant was in the front of the church or on the same side she was. What was that glint on the floor? She had to find out before someone else noticed it.

She nudged Hick, who was standing next to her waiting for his cue to move to the front to say his lines as the innkeeper. "Play along, and when it happens, carry me to the pew by the heart and then accidentally, gently drop me on the floor by the carved heart."

Mr. Warbler nudged her. "Quit talking. You will get us in trouble with Nellie. You are supposed to be singing."

"What?" Hick had been concentrating on the song and running his lines over in his mind, so Jezabelle's request confused him.

"Just do what I said. Now!" Jezabelle gave a loud swoon and dropped into Hick's arms. Everyone quit singing as they watched Hick lift Jezabelle up.

"She just fainted. It's fine," Hick assured the others.

Jezabelle lifted her head up. "Yes, I am just a little woozy from too much baking today and not enough eating. I just need to lie down for a minute."

Hick made his way across the church and over by the heart.

"Now," Jezabelle whispered before Hick tried to put her down in the pew nearest the heart.

Hick pretended to lose his balance and gently went down with Jezabelle on the floor next to the heart.

Hank and her friends rushed to help.

Jezabelle whispered to Hick as they lay on the floor, as she desperately looked around for the glinting object. "I said to drop me, not to come along with me."

Hick looked into her eyes. "I was afraid you would get hurt."

Hank was upon them helping Hick off of Jezabelle. "Are you hurt, Jezabelle? Are you okay?"

Jezabelle felt something hard underneath her. "I just need a minute for the dizziness to pass, and I will be fine. Let me lie here a second before I get up." She put her hand underneath her, grabbing the hard object under her stomach. Clutching it in her hand, she slid it into the same pocket with her rings and kept her hand on it so it didn't fall out when she stood up.

Reaching out her other hand to Hank, she said, "You can help me up now."

Hank reached down and lifted her up in his arms.

Jezabelle's cheeks turned red. "Put me down HH. I am fine, but if Lizzy would accompany me to the ladies' room, I would appreciate it. Continue on with your practice."

Lizzy quickly stepped forward. "You heard the lady, Hank. Set her down and I will help her to the ladies' room."

Hick said, "Yes, this happens when she doesn't eat and cooks all day. We need to make sure she takes better care of herself."

Hank reluctantly lowered Jezabelle so she could sit down in the church pew.

"Yes, after the ladies' room, I think I will have Lizzy take me over to the bistro and eat something. Let's go, Lizzy." Jezabelle stood up.

Lizzy took the arm that wasn't stuck in her dress. "I'll keep you informed." Leaning over, she whispered to Miranda who just reached the scene. "See you in the morning. Tell everyone to come in their pj's. I've heard Warbler wears some interesting ones."

Chapter Twenty-Seven

Jezabelle unlocked the door to the bistro and held it open for Lizzy. She turned both ways, scouring the street with her eyes to see if they were being watched. Stepping into the bistro, she turned and locked the door.

"Jezabelle, you are acting strangely. What is going on?"

Jezabelle motioned Lizzy over to the bar.

"Shouldn't we turn on a light?"

"No, we don't want anyone to know we are here," Jezabelle answered.

"They already know we are here because we said we were coming here," Lizzy reminded her.

"But he doesn't know we are here."

"He who?" Lizzy frowned. "Maybe we should go over to urgent care at the hospital. You may have bumped your head, and you are worse than I thought."

Jezabelle pulled her hand out of her pocket and plunked something down on the bar.

Lizzy peered through the darkness. "What is that?" She picked it up. "It's a glass cube. Is it like the others? We need light." She pulled out her cell phone and switched on the flashlight.

Jezabelle grabbed the cube out of her hand and put it in the beam of the light. "It is and look. It says, Melchior. It's the cube from the window at the bank. We have the three clues."

"But how did you get it? Was that fainting an act?"

"It was. I saw it glinting on the floor by the heart. I wasn't sure what it was, but they keep the floors spiffy and shiny in that church and I had to see what was sparkling before anyone else did."

Lizzy examined the cube closer. "But how did it get there?"

"I think the homeless man had it and accidentally dropped it," Jezabelle concluded. "I don't know where he disappeared to, but that is where I saw him standing."

"Why would a homeless man steal a piece of the window of the bank?"

"I don't know, but is it a coincidence he showed up about the same time Elfy was killed and we started finding the cubes and a new puzzle?"

"Do you really think this is a puzzle? That is pretty farfetched." Lizzy reminded her.

"Well, so was the floornapper caper."

A pounding on the door interrupted their conversation.

"Let me in. I know you are in there." Snoop Steckle hollered through the closed door.

"Snoop is pounding on the bistro door?" Jezabelle looked at Lizzy. "Quick, hide the cube somewhere until we can give it to Miranda to hide with the others."

Lizzy giggled as the pounding continued. "It might be Snodley, although I don't think conservative Snodley the reporter would be pounding on the door. Yup, it must be Snoop. Maybe Snoop overcame Snoodley. Whoops. I mean Snodley."

"I guess we will find out." Jezabelle checked to make sure Lizzy was off hiding the cube before she opened the door.

"Excuse me, but I thought I could grab a cuppa on this cold night," Snodley declared.

"You can grab a cuppa of something," Jezabelle declared. "But it might be a cuppa cahoots." She gave him a sharp look.

"My dear woman. You question a hardnosed reporter like Snodley?"

"Can it, Snoop. Snodley would not have tried to break down the door to get a scoop, but Snoop would have," Jezabelle informed him.

"Fine, fine. I am Snoop. What did you find at the church?"

"And why should I tell you?"

"Because I know the Discombobulated Decipherers—great name, by the way—are on to something, and it might have something to do with Elfy's murder and another puzzle," Snoop declared.

Lizzy walked back into the room just in time to hear Snoop's statement. "And you know this how, and why the Snodley persona?"

"And we don't know we are on to something so how could you?" Jezabelle quizzed.

"Because I am the one that got locked in the box by the homeless man, and he threatened my life if I told someone, so I decided to become my twin brother," Snoop answered.

"You have a twin brother?" Lizzy asked.

"Crackpot reporter for the London Times. He broke a story on espionage and was caught in the crossfire. He retired from reporting and is backpacking around the world, staying out of the limelight. No one's heard from him for years except me. He is the one who gave me the idea of amnesia and a different personality to keep myself safe."

"Why didn't you tell Hank?" Jezabelle asked.

"Because I want the story, and I kind of like staying alive. Once we solve it, I will go back to being lovable Snoop Steckle."

"The lovable part is your opinion," Jezabelle quipped.

"You think the homeless man is dangerous?" Lizzy asked.

"Well, he locked me in that bench and all because I found a glass cube stuffed inside it. He took the glass cube and threatened my life if I told anyone about it, and then he locked me inside after hitting me over the head. I call that dangerous, and now George, the custodian of the church, has disappeared. I think George found something out, so he did George in," Snoop explained.

Jezabelle began to pace the floor. "Maybe Ernest the elf is part of this. After all, he came to town to Santa's village, and this was all about the same time as the homeless man appeared and we found the glass cubes."

"What about Santa? He is not our usual fireman Santa. Where did he come from, and who hired him?" Lizzy asked.

"Why did we have someone from outside come in and play Santa?" Snoop asked.

"You're the snoop. Go and find out," Jezabelle challenged. "We have enough on our plate. Look, rehearsal is over. Miranda will be going to Fuchsia and Rack's for a late-night meal with Fleck. Turn out your flashlight. We don't want anyone to know we are still here."

"We have to stay here all night?" Snoop asked, alarmed.

Lizzy and Jezabelle exchanged a glance.

"Should we let him use our back door?" Jezabelle suggested.

"Back door? You have a back door?" Snoop asked.

"Well, not exactly, but it's up to code because there always has to be another way out. Follow us." Lizzy started toward the basement door.

"You're taking me to the basement... the basement?"

"Yup, no one will be the wiser." Jezabelle winked at Snoop.

Snoop held back. "Ah... I guess I will wait here until morning. Perhaps I was just dreaming with everything I said earlier." He peered past Jezabelle into the darkened basement and began to back up toward the front door.

Since we don't want anyone to see the basement light, I guess I will use my flashlight." She switched the cell phone flashlight on and pointed it down into the darkness.

"Come on, Snoop. We'll take care of you." Jezabelle grabbed his arm and propelled him forward.

"Ah, that's Snodley remember? Snodley. I don't know who Snoop is," he said nervously as Jezabelle led him down the darkened steps.

"Did you remember to put the Not Open Until Ten sign on the door, Jezabelle?" Lizzy yelled back through the darkness.

"You're not opening until ten? Where are you taking me?" Snoop whispered in the darkness.

Chapter Twenty-Eight

Jezabelle was sipping her coffee on Lizzy's couch when the others arrived. It was 5:03 a.m. Jezabelle spent the night at Lizzy's so she didn't have to go back out in the cold to get to her house when they got back home the evening before. Instead of sleeping, they spent the night planning the impromptu wine and dine they were holding that night.

Phoebe entered first, wearing a one-piece fleece jumpsuit in red, complete with feet attached. Warbler had on his footed pajamas. Hick arrived next, wearing his usual garb for cooking in the bistro.

Jezabelle and Lizzy held back their laughter when they first spied Phoebe.

"Don't say it. I didn't wear these to bed. You know what I wear to bed since you surprised me when you checked on me to see if I was dead. Since I had to go out in the cold, I pulled these out of the cedar chest. I wore them one year when I was a she-devil at Halloween, and it's cold out. You didn't think I was going to go out in my flimsies, did you?" Phoebe huffed.

"That's cheating. I wore what I usually wear," Warbler accused.

"And we already knew that, Warby." Lizzy stood up and grabbed his arm. "Let's go in the kitchen and get the sweets and coffee."

"Where is Miranda?" Hick asked.

"Where are your pj's?" Jezabelle countered.

"I thought I would go in early after our little meeting and get started on preparations for tonight. Have you got the menu ready? Plus we have the noon crowd you know?" Hick reminded them.

Miranda came in the door. She was dressed in fuzzy, teddy bear bottoms and a pink feathery pajama top. Her hair was mussed as she hadn't combed it before leaving her house.

"Where are your pajamas?" Miranda asked Hick.

Hick stared at Miranda, thinking she looked adorable. He stammered. "I-I-I have... to... work."

Jezabelle laughed at Hick's nervousness. "Miranda, did you have a nice night in Fuchsia with Fleck?"

"I did. Rack's restaurant has wonderful food. We ran into your niece Delight and her friend Hermiony."

"You ran into Granny? You have to watch out for that woman. She gets Delight into too much trouble. Did you learn anything from Fleck?" Jezabelle asked.

"I did. He said the mayor hired Santa this year. The mayor felt the kids were getting too smart these days and he wanted someone that wasn't from town so the little kids didn't recognize him. Apparently, last year one of the five-year-olds called Santa by his name. It seems he recognized him from the tour the little ones had of the firehouse. The fireman was the one who led the tour. It almost ruined Christmas for the wee ones."

"That a lot of 'I did,'" Hick said. "You didn't say any 'I do's' when you were with him?"

"Of course not, Hickory, it was the first date. Or was it a second? Who can keep track when you are with such a charming man," Miranda teased.

Hick glared at her.

"Here we are with coffee and Lemon Love Notes." Lizzy and Mr. Warbler entered the room both smiling like a Cheshire cat.

"You look like you have recovered from your faint last night," Phoebe said.

Hick answered before Jezabelle could open her mouth, "Yes, she got glassy all right."

"Were you drinking?" Phoebe's voice held a haughty tone.

"No, I wasn't drinking; I was pouncing on a clue."

"She found our third missing block, the one from the bank," Lizzy explained.

"Yes, it was by the wall with the heart in the church. I saw it glinting, and I wanted to get to it before anyone else. So I fainted and snatched it up, just like that." Jezabelle snapped her fingers.

"Where is it?" Mr. Warbler glanced around the room, looking for it.

"I hid it at the bistro. Snodley or Snoop interrupted us as we were pondering the clue," Jezabelle answered.

Lizzy continued. "Yes, he fessed up. He is pretending to be his brother because he is afraid instead of being stuffed into a seat he will be stuffed into a coffin next if they know he remembers."

"It's time to put our thinking caps on," Jezabelle said as she took a bite of her tart. First, Snoop Steckle is really Snoop, but he is pretending to be his twin brother Snodley because he is afraid the homeless man will attack him again."

"The homeless man? He attacked Snoop and put him in the seat in the back of the stable?" Phoebe shook her head. "I haven't even seen the homeless man yet."

Lizzy continued. "He claims he found the glass block in the bench and the homeless man hit him over the head, stole it from him, and then stuffed him in the bench."

"But how did Snoop know the block was there, and how did he know to look for the entrance to the box?" Hick pondered.

"We didn't ask him that, but I think we should," Jezabelle said.

"Yes, our brains were still on the fact that Jezabelle found one of the blocks in the church last night, and that is why she had Hick drop her on the floor. We think the homeless man dropped it earlier." Lizzy continued the story.

"It must be the same block that got stolen from the bank and from Snoop," Phoebe guessed.

A flash of light came through the darkness.

"What was that?" Phoebe ran to the window. "It's Snoop, but he's getting in his car. It's too late to catch him."

"If he is pretending to be Snodley, why is he taking a picture of us?" Miranda asked. "We aren't even doing anything this time."

Jezabelle shook her head. "He knows we know he is Snoop and that we will keep his secret for a short time until we figure this out. And being Snoop, I would guess our picture would show up somewhere anonymously because he is again snooping on us."

"What?" Phoebe jumped up and looked at her garb. "He can't publish a picture of me in this. I'll never live it down."

"Relax, Phoebe. Let's get back to deciphering what we know," Lizzy reminded her.

Mr. Warbler was stuffing another tart into his mouth. He wiped his chin and said, "We need to find this homeless man and interrogate him."

"Interrogate? You've been reading too many mysteries lately. Police interrogate, we cajole," Jezabelle said.

"You all decide whether you are going to interrogate or cajole. Someone has to run the bistro while all of you are being detectives. I'm going to work." Hick glowered at Miranda before leaving.

"Why is he glowering at me?" Miranda asked after he left. She threw her hands in the air.

Lizzy answered, a twinkle in her eye, "He has his shorts in a knot over your dinner last night."

Jezabelle thought she should change the subject. "We need to figure out if Santa is a part of this. Maybe he offed Ernest. He was following the homeless man the other night."

"Have you found George yet, Warbler?" Phoebe asked.

Mr. Warbler shook his head. "No, he has disappeared off the face of the earth or at least this part of the earth."

"And why kill Ernest? He wasn't that bad; he just had a liking for the women." Phoebe stated the fact.

"Why don't you talk to Hank, Jezabelle? See if he knows anything about this homeless man and tell him what we know," Lizzy suggested.

"Absolutely not! I am not talking to Hank and that's that!" Jezabelle stomped her foot on the floor to make her point.

Warbler and Lizzy's eyes skewered Jezabelle before exchanging glances between themselves.

Mr. Warbler cleared his throat nervously before speaking. "I see. Well... um, we should talk to the mayor and see if we can find this homeless man. Does everyone agree?" He glanced at Jezabelle to see if her mood had changed.

After a few more cups of coffee, Miranda set down her cup and announced, "It's time for us to get to work."

Jezabelle's cell phone rang. She picked up the phone, nodding her head. Ending the connection, she turned to the others. "We better get dressed and get to the bistro, Lizzy. Hick said someone broke in. I guess I'll have to talk to HH as Hick called the police."

Chapter Twenty-Nine

Hank Hardy, Hanna Hardy, and Stick Straight were milling around the bistro when Jezabelle and Lizzy dashed in from the basement, having used the tunnel from Lizzy's house.

"Where are Miranda, Phoebe, and Warbler?" Hick asked, noticing the two were alone. "I thought for sure they would get here faster than you."

"They are home changing clothes. We had our clothes with us, or at least I have last night's clothes since I didn't take the time to go home," Jezabelle explained.

"Jezzy, do you have any idea who might have wanted to break into the bistro?" Hank was still taking notes as he questioned her."

"Is anything missing?" Jezabelle asked Hick.

Hick shook his head. "It doesn't seem to be. The place is just a mess. Sugar tossed out of the canisters, flour on the floor, and they even dug through the ice cream containers. It doesn't look like they wanted to eat it, just thought something might have been hiding in it."

Hanna gave Jezabelle a keen look. "Is there anything you are keeping from us?"

The three of Brilliant's finest waited for her to answer.

Lizzy stepped forward. "We are in the dark too. We were closed for practice last night and decided to open late this morning because we are having a party tonight or—we were."

"We're through here," Stick Straight piped up. "If you can't find anything stolen, then it looks like a routine break-in and they didn't find anything they wanted unless they were trying to steal Jezabelle's delicious donuts. They didn't get to the basement since the door to the basement was locked."

Jezabelle closed the door after Hank, Hanna, and Stick left. She turned to Lizzy. "They must have been after the glass block. Where is it? Where did you hide it?"

Lizzy scurried around to the back of the bar and knelt down on the floor. She felt the wood molding at the bottom of the bar. When she found the hidden lever neatly concealed in the wood, she moved it aside, and part of the molding fell open. She removed the glass cube.

"Wow. I didn't know that was there. How did you know that was there?" Jezabelle bent down to examine the opening.

"It was an accident," Lizzy explained. "When I was polishing the molding on this old bar, my cloth caught on something. I thought it was a sliver of wood, but it wouldn't come out, and that is when I realized if I moved it sideways, it opened this hidden door. I guess another of the Brilliant brothers' puzzles or their sense of humor."

"We better get this mess cleaned up. It's a good thing we aren't opening until later." Hick picked up a broom.

"I will finalize the menu for tonight and check on the wine to make sure we have enough for an impromptu event. It will be nice when we get the basement turned into a full-time venue so we don't have to keep converting this space." Lizzy disappeared through the basement door.

"I better get the coffee going and the muffins in the oven." Hick glanced out the front window. "I think Santa wants some coffee before he heads toward the square."

Jezabelle, hiding the glass cube again in the bottom of the bar, raised her head to peek out just as a light tap sounded on the door. "I guess we can let him in. We might learn something." She got up and went around the bar to unlock the door.

"I see you are not open until ten today, but I was wondering if I could get a cup of coffee to take with me to my Santa chair. It's a little nippy out there and slippery. You might want to put some deicer on your sidewalk." Santa stomped his feet outside the door so he wouldn't carry the snow into the bistro.

"You can sit if you want," Jezabelle answered. "We are opening later so we could get ready for tonight, but we had an unexpected visitor and we have cleanup duty."

Santa's frown could be seen behind his beard. "Someone broke into the bistro?"

"They sure did," Hick answered, setting a cup of dark coffee down in front of Santa. "Freshly brewed."

"Aren't you starting a little early this morning?" Jezabelle asked while studying Santa's face to see if she could guess if she knew the person under the Santa suit.

"Well, you know those kids around Christmas time; they get up early, and today will be busy since tomorrow is the Christmas pageant. Not much time to make sure I know what they want."

Jezabelle saw the bistro door open and the homeless man put one foot inside the business. Suddenly he pulled his foot back out the door, turned, and left.

"That's interesting," Jezabelle remarked.

"What's that?" Hick asked, handing Jezabelle a cup of brew.

Nodding toward the door, Jezabelle answered, "The homeless man—he was about to come in, and then he quickly turned around and left."

Santa's head came up. He set his coffee down, threw some money on the counter, stood up, and said, "I have to go. Ho! Ho! Ho!" And he almost ran out the door.

Frowning, Hick remarked, "He seemed in a hurry."

"I might be imagining things, but I think he is going after the homeless man." Jezabelle moved to hawk out the window to see if she could still see them. "They are both gone, quick as the wind."

Turning toward Hick, she asked, "Throw me my coat. Can you hold down the fort for a little while? I have an errand to run."

Hick grabbed her coat off the counter where she had thrown it and tossed it to her. "Since the doors don't open until ten this morning, we have plenty of time. We should still be good to go tonight. Where are you going?"

"I had a quick question for Santa, so I thought I would go over to the town square after him. I'll be right back," she said as she opened the door and stepped into the cold.

Chapter Thirty

Jezabelle looked back to make sure Hick wasn't watching from the bistro. Instead of going all the way to the center of the town square, she zipped around the side of the church to the back door. She hoped it wasn't locked.

Looking toward Pastor Sifter and Nellie's house to make sure all was quiet, she tried the back door of the church. It was open. Quietly she stepped into the still, dark hall. Feeling her way to the stairway, she grabbed the railing. Jezabelle saw there was no light in the church. Quietly she climbed the steps to the church proper.

When she reached the top of the steps, she moved into the shadowy church. Her eyes adjusted to the dim light. The sun was coming up and shining a small glow through the stained glass windows. She saw the spot across the church where she found the glass block. Weaving her way across through the pews, she stopped by the wall where the large heart was carved. She felt along the wall. It seemed to be solid.

Giving up, she turned and eyed the rest of the church, resting against the carved heart. Suddenly it moved inward, taking her with it as she fell backward.

Just as she was prepared to hit the ground, she felt arms catch her and pull her farther back, dragging her away from the heart, which had swung inward.

Jezabelle found herself staring into the face of the homeless man. "You!"

He quickly set her down on a small bed and moved to close the heart and seal the wall again.

Jezabelle stood up. "I knew you were up to no good. You had the glass block and lost it. Why is it so important?" Then realizing she was locked in a tiny room with no windows with the homeless man, she shouted, "They know I'm here. They will miss me and come looking, and then you'll be found out."

Another voice answered her outburst. "It's okay, Jezabelle, and no one will hear you. He won't hurt you. At least I don't think he will. He's treated me well."

Jezabelle turned around. "George, you're here. This is where you disappeared." She walked up and touched the missing custodian's face.

"Yes, um, I had to delay George for a little while so he wouldn't tell anyone that I built the bench chest in the stable."

"And knocked out Snoop?" Jezabelle added.

"Yes, well, that was unfortunate. He found the glass block I had stuffed inside there when I was spying on the community. Come now, sit down and I will explain." The homeless man reached to touch Jezabelle's arm.

Jezabelle shrugged away from the grasp. "Don't touch me, you... you... perpetrator."

George tapped Jezabelle on her shoulder. "Really I don't think he would hurt you. Maybe you should listen to him."

"Maybe you are in on this, George, and want me to think otherwise," she accused the custodian.

"No, I just want to get out of here in time for the pageant."

"Did you know this hidden room was here, George?" Jezabelle moved to examine the walls.

"No, it's well hidden. I didn't know until I woke up inside here."

"He kidnapped you?" Jezabelle gave the homeless man the evil eye, skewering him with a scowl.

"Okay, that's enough. Both of you settle down," The homeless man instructed. "I need you to call whomever has the three glass blocks and get them to deliver them to us."

"And then what? You knock us off? You stick it to us? You make us walk the plank and then you shuffle off to Buffalo?"

The homeless man's face broke into a large grin, and he began to laugh. "No, but those are great ideas."

Seeing the smile on the homeless man's face, Jezabelle began to smile too. "I guess those are possibilities, but I warn you before you consider them, consider this. Hank Hardy will be looking for me if he doesn't get his cheesecake today. And he'll find us and arrest you."

Jezabelle felt a tap on her shoulder. "I don't mean to interrupt, but no one has found me, and at first I yelled the church down and no one heard me." George lifted his arms in a hopeless gesture and sat down on the cot in the corner of the room.

"I guess the jig's up. Maybe you can help me. Sit down and I will tell you all." The homeless man indicated Jezabelle should join George on the bed.

"First did you kill Elfy?" Jezabelle crossed her arms and tapped her toe.

"No, I didn't kill him, although I knew him. In fact, he got to Brilliant first and found the first block, and I suspect you may know where that one is."

"And why should we believe you?" George asked.

"Because all I want is to find the answer to the puzzle of my family. That is why I am here. My name is Disaster Darling."

Jezabelle glanced at George and saw he was trying to keep from laughing. "You think we are going to believe your name is Disaster?"

The homeless man sighed. "My full name is Disaster Brilliant Darling. Use it in a sentence, like this: 'Disaster? Brilliant, darling.' My parents and grandparents had quite the imagination. My mother had a flair for the dramatic. The story that was told to me is right after I was born, the hospital caught on fire. It was a disaster. My mother's maiden name was Brilliant, and my mother always called my father darling, so instead of them giving me his last name on my birth certificate, which was Podunk, they decided to change their last name to darling too after my father suggested the name Disaster because of the fire. My mother said, 'Disaster, brilliant, darling,' and I became Disaster Brilliant Darling." He looked at Jezabelle's and George's faces and saw their mouths had dropped open. "I know it is hard to believe."

"So you are a descendant of the Brilliant brothers who founded this community?" Jezabelle asked.

"Yes, only I just found that out a few months ago after my parents died. My mother was a great-granddaughter of Broderick Brilliant. At least I think so. I found some old papers and a journal up in the attic of my parents' house. They lived in a rural area of Oregon."

"Are you really homeless?" George asked.

"Well, I'm not rich, but I get by and I have a home, and I decided the best way for people not to ask questions was to come to Brilliant as a homeless man. People tend to want to avoid those who are tattered and appear to not have a home. They don't know what to say to them."

"Where does Ernest the elf come into this? You said you knew him?" Jezabelle asked.

"Yes, he was the groundskeeper for my parents' house. Once they got older, they couldn't keep the place up and I lived overseas, so they hired Ernest. He worked for them a long time. But he disappeared soon after I came to tidy up their estate. I suspect he found the journal and stole some pages out of it," Disaster explained.

"Why don't you just come out with it and tell us what the papers said." Frustration tinged Jezabelle's voice.

"It had the story of the building of this church and the death of Broderick's daughter, Belle, and the bell tower that was sealed up. In their heartbreak, their surprise for their daughter—and they called it a treasure—was sealed up in that bell tower. They left a puzzle for their descendants in case anyone wanted to know the full story. That's how I found this room and the fact the heart was a puzzle piece. One glass block was supposed to be in an indentation in the side of the heart when the door swung inward. Only it was missing." Disaster shook his head. "I think Ernest found it first. And I think he has the other part of the architect plans for this church, only now he is dead and I don't know where he might have hidden them."

"I clean this church every day. I dust the walls, and the heart never swung inward for me," George remarked, moving over to examine the hinges that could only be seen from inside the room.

Disaster held up a flat item the size of a playing card. "It's a magnet. You place it half on the side of the heart and half on the brick adjoining it, and it releases the lock and the heart loosens so you can push it open. It was genius for them to invent this back in those days."

"How did you get the magnet?" Jezabelle asked.

"It was with the papers and the book and an architectural drawing."

"And don't you think we would have noticed the glass block stuck in the wall?" George pointed out.

"If you walk past something every day, how often do you actually take a close look at the familiar scenery?" Disaster reminded them. "Whatever is on the other half must not have needed the magnet, or Ernest overlooked it. The other half of the drawing must have had a more valuable puzzle. Did you know my ancestors were puzzle makers?"

Jezabelle laughed and patted Disaster on the shoulder. "We did. We sure did."

Chapter Thirty-One

"Let me go and I will bring you the glass block," Jezabelle suggested.

"And let you bring the police and that Santa to find me? I think not." Disaster crossed his arms in front of him and planted his feet firmly on the ground.

Jezabelle frowned. "What does Santa have to do with this? I did notice you were avoiding him."

"Does he look familiar to you, Jezabelle?" George joined the conversation.

"He seems to be following me. Do you know who he really is?" Disaster asked.

Jezabelle shook her head. "He seems familiar, but why would he follow you?"

"All I can figure out is that he is looking to solve the puzzle of the cubes too. And what they are leading us to." Jezabelle was silent for a moment before going up on her tiptoes and putting her face right in front of Disaster's, looking him in the eyes. "Did you break into the bistro?"

"Break into the bistro? No. I wouldn't do something like that."

"You kidnapped me. And now you kidnapped Jezabelle, and you wouldn't break into the bistro?" George tongue twisted around his words.

"I might have, but someone beat me to it. Now, Jezabelle, I assume you and the discombobulated ones have all three cubes. I want you to call your friend Lizzy and tell her to bring them to you here at the church. And to make sure no one follows her." Disaster continued his instructions. "Tell her it's all figured out, but you want to run it past her before you tell the others."

"Did you know Nellie Sifter knows the story of the Bell Tower, and she and Pastor Sifter are planning on building a new tower so they can have a working bell? She found the pages stuffed under the baptismal urn. I take it you didn't put them there." Jezabelle stalled for time.

"I didn't. I think Ernest hid them there before he met his demise."

"Do you suppose she might have the other half of the church's building plans?" George asked.

"I don't think so. According to Jackson Ritter, she was pretty forthcoming about the information she found." Jezabelle still stalled, hoping to keep Disaster from implementing the next phase of his plan until she could figure out her next step.

"Enough. Call your friend Lizzy. Then give me your phone."

Jezabelle pulled her cell phone out of her pocket. She pulled up Lizzy's number and poked the dot on the screen to place the call.

"Lizzy, don't let Hick hear this call. Send him down to the Brilliant BeDazzle Brewery to borrow some wine for tonight. Something we don't have. Then dig out the glass block. When Hick gets back, go to Miranda's house and tell her I want to hide the three blocks in the same place and have her give you the ones she has. Then make sure no one is following you, and bring them to the church and meet me by the baptismal fountain. And don't tell anyone. I think I have the solution, but I don't want to tell the others until I am sure." Jezabelle glanced at Disaster, but seeing he was standing right next to her, she waited for Lizzy's answer and then hung up before trying to give Lizzy a clue that she was in trouble.

Disaster patted her on the back. "You can keep your phone. I trust you now."

Jezabelle rolled her eyes. "Well, I don't trust you. Tell me something. What are we doing with the blocks when we get them? And why do they have the name of the Three Wise Men on them?"

"I don't know. That is what we are going to figure out." Disaster moved to the edge of the room and pushed aside an old picture on the wall. Behind the picture was a squared-out indentation that was built in the wall. He took out a small journal that sat in the small cubby. This says the key is with Balthazar, Melchior, and Gaspar."

"That could mean anything. The Three Wise Men are on the opposite wall of this church. There are three wise men in the nativity scene outside," George countered.

"And Miranda has a nativity scene carved into the wall of her basement. That is where she found her block," Jezabelle added before frowning. "But what about the glass block in the bank window? That's not a nativity scene." Her eyes got wide. "You broke the bank window," she accused Disaster.

He looked sheepish. "Aw, indeed I did. I felt bad about that, but I happened to be out walking at night when I saw your friend Lizzy stop by and look for something with her spyglass and flashlight. After she left, I went over to see what interested her and saw the block. I knew I had to get it before you and your decipherers came back to look at it again and before whoever else is involved in all of this got to it. So I smashed and separated."

"And then you dropped it and I found it," Jezabelle concluded. Disaster nodded in agreement.

George asked, "Can I go once you have the glass blocks if I decide to be quiet. There is so much to do with the Christmas pageant tomorrow night."

"We'll see. I really don't want to hurt you. Maybe we can have this all wrapped up before Christmas," Disaster speculated.

"If you let me bring in all the Discombobulated Decipherers, we might be able to do that. We are pretty good at putting the puzzle together, but we have to do it so HH and the rest of the force don't get wind of it, or they will stop us and you possibly will be arrested for Ernest's murder because you had a motive," Jezabelle suggested.

"I didn't murder Ernest. Whatever the treasure is in this church, I would have shared with him. He was a faithful employee of my parents."

"Do you have any other ancestors alive?" George queried. "We seem to have met a few of them lately and they brought mayhem to town."

"I don't know. There were just my parents and me. They didn't talk about their family, but maybe they didn't know much about their grandparents. They certainly never said anything. Enough about this. Your friend Lizzy should be here soon, and I have to watch for her."

Chapter Thirty-Two

The hidden heart door swung inward, and Snoop Steckle stumbled into the room after being pushed by Disaster.

"Snoop, what are you doing here?" Jezabelle asked while helping him up off the floor.

"He was outside with his camera flashing a picture when I was sneaking out the door. Hold on to him until I get your friend Lizzy." The door closed, cutting off his instructions.

"I knew it. I knew it. That homeless man killed Ernest the elf and then he stuffed me into the box so I wouldn't let people know he was spying on them from the box," Snoop sputtered.

"He could have killed you, Snoop, but he didn't. I don't think he killed Ernest, but the jury's not in yet. What are you doing here?" Jezabelle brushed off his red suit.

Instead of answering Jezabelle, Snoop stared at George. "George, you're alive. You're here. Is he in on this?"

"No, I'm not in on this whatever this is. I just got put in here too so I wouldn't talk," George answered.

Snoop looked around the room. "Where is here? I didn't know there was a hidden room in the church."

"No one did. Disaster found it from a drawing of the church. He's really not homeless, and his name is Disaster Brilliant Darling," Jezabelle explained.

Snoop hesitated before answering, "This is a joke right? No one names their kid Disaster let alone Brilliant Darling."

"Well, his parents did." George laughed. "It's like this. When he was born, the suggestion was to name him Disaster because something about his birth was a disaster. His dad's name was Podunk, and his mother said, "Disaster, brilliant, darling." And then it dawned on them it would be the perfect name because Brilliant was her maiden name. It sounded like the brilliant thing to do. And they liked the name Darling better than Podunk, so they changed their name."

The door swung open, and Disaster and Lizzy entered. Disaster closed the door after them. "I'm sorry I had to grab you, Lizzy, but you were going to scream when I tried to talk you into coming with me."

"Indeed I was. Come on, Jezabelle, let's scream together. I'm sure someone will eventually hear us. What is this place? George, why are you here? And Snoop? Oh my, did you solve the puzzle because all these guys are in on it and they caught you and now we are hostages?" Lizzy babbled.

"Well yes and no," Jezabelle answered. "George is an innocent bystander. Snoop is a nosy snoop like he always has been, and Disaster is a relative of the Brilliant brothers, and no, before you ask, he says he did not kill Elfy and I believe him. George is still alive, and I must say I have a hard time keeping my hands off Snoop, so that was the test. Snoop is still alive."

"You'd kill me?" Snoop gasped.

"Did you bring the glass cubes?" Disaster asked.

Lizzy pulled them out of her purse.

Jezabelle watched as Disaster took them from Lizzy and examined each one. "Do you see anything we didn't see?"

He shook his head. They look like plain glass cubes to me. They certainly aren't crystal. You might think that was the reason the Brilliant brothers hid them around. If they were crystal, they might have had value, but they are a heavy glass. They aren't even totally clear."

"Can we leave now?" Lizzy asked, inching toward the wall with the door.

"No, not yet. I'll let you all go when I have this solved." Disaster turned one block over and over in his hand.

Jezabelle stepped forward. "You need the Discombobulated Decipherers. We won't tell HH and the rest of the deputies because they are busy with the murder and this appears to be a puzzle, and I am sure Hank isn't interested. Why don't we make a deal with Snoop that he gets the scoop if he keeps quiet, and I am sure George just wants to get out of here to prepare for the pageant? He's never been a tattletale, right George?"

George cleared his throat. "Right. If you knew what I knew from cleaning this hallowed hall... well, you would be shocked. But I look at myself the same way a priest looks at confession. I can't reveal anything even under the threat of death."

Disaster glared at Snoop. "Well, Snodley, Snooper, or whatever, if I let you go and you breathe a word of this to anyone, you will be sealed in a box forever. You sure had me going with that Snodley thing. You should be an actor."

Snoop turned white and stammered. "I... ah... will wait for word from you." He turned to Jezabelle. "You promise I get the scoop?"

Disaster peered out a small hole in the door that the others hadn't noticed. "The coast is clear."

"What, all this time we could have seen what was happening outside this wall?" Jezabelle crabbed.

Disaster smiled. "Yup, you can see out but not in. Clever thing because when this was built, they put a small tube through the door, and on the outside, it looks like a miniature heart inside the big one in the corner." He laughed. "Again you don't notice details about things you see every day because they become common."

He slid the door open. "The blocks are staying here for safekeeping. You can all leave. I expect all the Discombobulated Decipherers back here tonight. There is no practice since tomorrow is Christmas Eve and the pageant. The church should be clear. George, you can do your custodian duties tonight and keep others away."

"Got it, chief." George slid through the door. Snoop almost pushed him over for the chance to leave.

Jezabelle and Lizzy followed. "Midnight. No one should see us then. And keep the lights off. They've seen the lights on in the middle of the night."

"That wasn't me either. Perhaps it was that strange Santa who is always following me." Disaster closed the door before they could answer him.

Jezabelle frowned and turned to Lizzy. "Maybe we should be checking out Santa more closely. If he was interested in Disaster and Disaster is a Brilliant descendant, maybe Santa is the one who killed Ernest and is going to do the same thing to Disaster. Perhaps he is a long-lost Brilliant relative that they would recognize, so he donned a Santa suit to throw them off."

Lizzy shivered. "I am feeling déjà vu here from the last time we got involved in the floor napping. It almost got us killed. Maybe we should tell Hank. Or if we could find Rock, he could help us too. What's next?"

"We come back with the others tonight and read through this journal that Disaster has. A few pages are missing, and they are the ones Nellie found that explains the closed-off bell tower. Ernest left them because Ernest was an employee of Disaster's parents. It's a long story and I will fill you in, but we better get back and help Hick before he gets suspicious and comes looking for us."

"I'm confused," Lizzy commented. "Hick is part of us now and he'll find out anyway so what difference does it make if he comes looking for us?"

"He'd let my cheesecakes and muffins burn and for what, information that he would get anyway? Really, Lizzy, I just don't understand your reasoning of what is important in life." Jezabelle turned and flounced down the aisle of the church to the back narthex and out the front door. She yelled back, "And if anyone asks why we are in here, tell them we're praying for Phoebe and Sigfried that they don't kill each other during the pageant."

Chapter Thirty-Three

"Where have you been?" Hick demanded an answer when they arrived back at the bistro.

"I had to interview them," Snoop answered, following Jezabelle and Lizzy in the door of the bistro.

"And we ran into George getting ready for the pageant," Lizzy said on her way back to the kitchen.

"We will fill you in later. We are having a meeting of the Discombobulated Decipherers at the church at midnight. Can you call the others, Hick?" Jezabelle asked.

Hick stood up straight. "Since I need a break, why don't I just take a drive to your neighborhood and tell Miranda myself and she can let Phoebe and Warbler know. I will take her some muffins from you."

Jezabelle laughed. "You can do that if you are trying to find an excuse to visit Miranda, but make sure you get back here before the noon rush. No canoodling."

"Canoodling?" Hick wrinkled his nose. "I guess there won't be any canoodling since I don't know what that is."

"Youngsters," Lizzy commented. "What are you doing, Snoop?" She watched him examining the underside of the tables.

"I... ah... where did you hide the cube you had?"

Jezabelle, Lizzy, and Hick eyed the bent over Snoop.

"Snoop... are you the one who broke into the bistro?" Jezabelle moved closer to the reporter.

"I can explain. I can explain. I knew you were all at Lizzy's this morning. And I knew you wouldn't let me in on your secrets. I knew you had the glass block from the church. I am a reporter and observant, you know. I was curious as to why everyone wanted that glass block. After all, I got shoved into a bench because of it."

Lizzy handed Snoop a bucket and a floor cloth. "You can wash the floor since you dumped all our flour and sugar on the floor, and it better be done before the lunch crowd."

Jezabelle and Hick laughed.

"I'm out of here." Hick held up the bag with muffins.

"I guess I better get cooking. It's going to be a long day."

Chapter Thirty-Four

"Why are we here?" Warbler whispered as he tried to find his way into the dark church.

"Because Jezabelle has news. We are close to cracking this case." Miranda gave Warbler a little push so he would move faster.

"Stop it," Warbler ordered. "Do you want me tumbling down and breaking something and your having to call an ambulance, letting the entire community know we snuck into the church in the middle of the night?"

"Pipe down," Phoebe interjected. "I didn't see anyone following us and seeing us come into the church. Did you?"

"No, the coast is clear." Hick came up behind them with his cell flashlight shining toward the floor. "Why aren't you using your flashlights?"

"A good mystery writer doesn't need flashlights; she has intuition on the correct steps to take." Miranda grabbed his cell phone and turned the flashlight off. "You'll get used to the dark, and the moon is shining some light through the windows."

"I see you finally made it," Disaster's voice whispered in Phoebe's ear.

Phoebe jumped and was ready to scream when she felt a hand grab her arm.

"Shh, it's okay, Phoebe." Jezabelle's soft voice came in her other ear.

"Warbler, grab my hand. You all link hands, and grab Warby's hand and come with me."

Warbler, startled by an unseen entity grabbing his hand, jumped back. "Lizzy, where did you come from?" He took her hand.

Lizzy led the group through the pews over to the heart on the wall. Jezabelle and Disaster followed, still holding on to Phoebe.

"Step aside." Disaster moved to the wall and used the magnet to open the door.

Warbler, Hick, Phoebe, and Miranda gasped, but before they had more time to react, Lizzy pulled them through the door.

Disaster closed the door behind them and lit a hurricane lamp in the corner of the room. "There doesn't appear to be any electricity in this room, so I have been using an oil lamp."

"This is Disaster Brilliant Darling," Jezabelle announced.

Nervous laughs filled the room. "Yeah, right," Hick said.

"We're supposed to be quiet," Phoebe reminded them.

"It's fine. No one can hear you from here. George was held in this room for days, and we didn't hear him," Lizzy explained.

"And now we're here. We're here and we can't get out, and we are hostages and you put us in here. We thought we knew you, but you and Jezabelle appear to be in cahoots with this Disaster person, and we'll never get out and we'll die here. Did you murder Elfy? Was that the plan?" Phoebe rambled before getting right in front of Lizzy's face. "You. You! I always knew we couldn't trust you!"

Jezabelle laughed. "Down, Phoebe. None of us were in on anything except for Disaster here, and he has brought the Discombobulated Decipherers here to help."

"To help with what, offing another elf?" Phoebe countered.

Disaster here is a descendant of the Brilliant brothers, and when his parents died, he found a journal and papers that led him here to this church. Yes, he knew Ernest, but for some strange reason, I believe he didn't kill him because he didn't hurt George or me. I think we need to listen to him so we can solve our puzzle." Jezabelle's stern look held no patience for argument.

"Fine!" Phoebe flounced over and sat down on the cot. "Let's hear it!"

Disaster indicated with his arm the others should sit too. "I found this journal, but a couple of pages are torn out. I don't know what the puzzle leads to, but it has something to do with the death of Broderick's daughter, Belle, and this church. At least that is what I surmise from the pages I have in the journal. I also have half an architectural drawing of the church—the half this room is in—and that is how I found this room. I have no idea why this space was hidden, but it makes me very curious to know if the other side of the church holds secrets too.

"Adding to this mystery it is possible there is another Brilliant relative or bystander who found out about this secret, and they are the ones who murdered Ernest, or Ernest's murder might not be connected." Lizzy paced as she talked.

Miranda stood up and began to pace in the small room with Lizzy, causing Jezabelle and Disaster to sit down to get out of the way of their pacing.

"It seems highly unlikely from this mystery author's standpoint that there isn't a connection. After all, I murder people in my books and I would make a connection." Miranda stopped in front of Disaster. "So let's see this journal."

"Not until I know none of you are going to the police," Disaster warned.

"And spoil our fun?" Hick asked. "This is my first undercover subterfuge, and I don't want it spoiled by Chief Hank Hardy."

Mr. Warbler and Phoebe nodded in agreement.

Disaster stood up and moved to the picture on the wall, pushing it aside and taking the journal and the blocks out of his hiding place. He set the blocks on the floor in front of them. "Tell me what do you see?"

"The words Balthazar, Gaspar, and Melchior," Hick answered. "They are the names of the Three Wise Men.

"Three six-sided square two-by-two cubes made of glass," Phoebe mused.

"They appear to be clear, but you know what they say: appearances can be deceiving." Miranda leaned forward and picked one up. "It's strange, but it seems as if you should be able to peer through the glass and see the lettering from the other side, but you can't."

"One block was found in Miranda's nativity scene, another— the one you found Phoebe—was originally right here in this church in the stone by the heart." Jezabelle spoke her thoughts out loud. "And then, of course, we have the one that you stole, Disaster, which was in the window of the bank."

"You are the one who broke the bank window?" Mr. Warbler accused Disaster.

"He did. But now how do they all tie together, and why were they placed where they were by the Brilliant brothers?" Jezabelle continued.

"What I don't understand"—Miranda broke in—"is why are you hiding in this church, and why didn't you just come out and talk to people?"

"I got here after Ernest. I knew he stole the pages from the journal, and I found out he was dead and I didn't know if it had to do with the journal, so I decided to adopt the homeless persona. I found this room with my half of the architectural drawing and the instructions on it to open the door. I didn't want to be the next dead stiff, and then that crazy Santa started following me. I thought perhaps he is the one that offed Ernest," Disaster explained.

"You think Santa is in on this? Oh, this just gets better and better. Do you have a pen and paper that I can jot down ideas for my next book?" Miranda looked around the room to find a pen.

Jezabelle eyed Miranda. "Miranda, you haven't got our last adventure down yet since we gave you full rights to write about it. Let's get this solved first."

"So what is our next step? The pageant is tonight since it's after midnight now. That doesn't give us much time to snoop today," Phoebe reminded them.

"Well, let's look at the journal. This part intrigues me." Disaster read the passage. "Says the keys are with Balthazar, Melchior, and Jasper."

They all looked down at the glass blocks with the three names on them.

Hick frowned. "Does that mean there was a key hidden by where we found these?"

"A key to what?" Mr. Warbler asked.

Or does it mean the Three Wise Men that are carved into the church wall, the nativity scene in the square, or the Wise Men in Miranda's basement, or all three?" Lizzy continued the questions.

Jezabelle shook her head. "Are there any other Wise Men floating around on walls in this community or on display that we have missed?"

"A key to what?" Mr. Warbler asked again.

"Disaster, you have been watching the manger scene from the built-in box. Did you see anything to indicate the live nativity scene might have the answer?" Jezabelle tapped one of the blocks on the floor.

"No, and George built the door for the baby to stay in it today so I can't check it out from underneath again."

"I think we can rule anything out that isn't visible all year long. After all, whatever these clues are, they must be visible year round. That would only make sense," Miranda surmised.

"Since when does anything in this brilliant town make sense?" Hick threw up his arms in defeat.

"I still don't get the window in the bank. We thought it was the original window." Jezabelle's voice drifted on in thought. "I know! Miranda, you go home and examine your walls in your basement and see if you can find a key anywhere. Hick, talk to George and have him examine this wall under his custodian-dusting guise, and see if he can find a key hidden and disguised. And since Snoop knows about this, let's put him to work and have him do a story on the bank window that was broken."

"What? No! They might arrest me if there is a story." Disaster became agitated.

"No... he isn't going to really do a story until this is all done, but he can find out the history of the window. I know it's Christmas Eve, but we were all going to spend it together since we are all alone except for Phoebe with her mom and sister. We meet back here after the pageant and everyone has gone home. We'll have time before Christmas morning services to see what we came up with."

Phoebe raised her eyebrows. "I can come too. My mother and sister are on a cruise courtesy of me. When I found out they were both dating Ernest the elf, I decided they needed some new scenery in their lives—man scenery. They won't be back until after New Year's."

"One by one you can leave." Disaster moved to the door and peeked through the peephole. The coast is clear. Leave five minutes in between each of you leaving the church, and don't turn on any lights. Lights at night will arouse suspicion in this church, and they are already looking into the lights being on the night Ernest was killed."

"Jezabelle, what are you and Lizzy and Hick going to do? You gave us all a job," Miranda asked.

"We are going to run the bistro. It's Christmas Eve day and we serve Tom and Jerry's and our special Christmas melted candy cane cheesecake. We don't want anyone to be suspicious and we can keep an eye on Santa. Oh and Phoebe... do not let Sigfried distract you from your snoopy sleuthing."

Chapter Thirty-Five

"Santa, you are on time for your morning coffee. It's your last day here. Are all the good little boys and girls getting gifts under the tree tomorrow morning?" Lizzy poured the first cup of the day from the fresh blend of Holiday Cheer coffee.

"Ho, ho, ho. Even some bad little boys and girls will be getting a gift. I'm just a softy, and what better gift than a note from Santa believing they can be better. And Mrs. Claus will be happy to have me back home. Those elves have been giving her a tough time," he answered with a glint in his eye.

Jezabelle joined Lizzy behind the counter and looked straight into Santa's eyes. "And where might you call home, Santa?"

Santa paused before answering, "Ah, that is the mystery. Santa's home can be anywhere in your imagination. Near or far, believe and Santa can be where you are." With that, he got up and, taking the last drink of coffee, put his cup down on the bar and with a "Ho, ho, ho" exited the bistro.

Lizzy and Jezabelle looked at one another and both said at the same time, "I know him."

"Then who is he?" Hank came in the door.

They both shook their heads and again said at the same time, "We don't know."

"Then how do you know you know him?"

177

"It's a feeling," Jezabelle answered.

Hank laughed. "Tonight's the night. I have to thank you for getting me out of my comfort zone. I am enjoying leading the pageant, and I owe it all to you, Jezzy."

"I knew you could do it. That little snafu with the high school play happened a long time ago, and I hated to see such talent wasted. Was Hanna surprised?"

"She was. She has talent like her mom, but now she says she thinks she gets part of her musical abilities from me. Go figure. She also wonders what else I have hidden from her." Hank winked at Jezabelle, a sly smile on his face.

"That's right. You two used to run around together in high school," Lizzy commented.

Both Hank and Jezabelle laughed.

"It depends on what you mean by run around." Hank appeared to be studying his cup.

"Dating, you know, the kissy, kissy thing we all used to do in high school?"

"Well, Lizzy, that was a long time ago. Hank dated Hanna's mom for most of high school. Hank and I were just friends." Jezabelle had a wistful look in her eyes.

The door to the bistro opened, and Snoop dressed as Snodley came in. Lizzy and Jezabelle gave him a perplexed look.

"Well, Snodley, what brings you to the bistro on this Christmas Eve day? Are you ready for the pageant?" Hank turned to the man who had sat down on the stool beside him.

"Yes, Snodley, what brings you here?" Lizzy asked suspiciously.

"Well, my dear woman, I was told that Jezabelle here needed my opinion on her cheesecake and I could write a story about this bistro for the London Times."

"I did?" Oh... I did. Come into the kitchen, Snodley." Jezabelle gestured for him to follow her.

Once in the kitchen, Snoop said, "What do you need, Jezabelle? Are we ready to solve the puzzle and I get the story?"

"What is up with the Snodley thing?"

"Everyone else still thinks I am Snodley. We don't want to tell them. They treat me with more respect and flock to me for stories. What gives?"

"Okay, Snoop or Snodley, we need you to go to the bank and interview Hutchinson Bellamy about the history of that window. Find out if it is original or how the blocks came to be. Something is off with finding the block there. And it has to be done now. Report back to me this afternoon." Jezabelle gave him a push through the door of the kitchen.

He turned back and whispered, "And then I get the story?"

"When it is said and done, Snodley, when it is said and done."

Chapter Thirty-Six

Jezabelle quit singing and listened as the cast and congregation finished the Christmas pageant with a hearty rendition of "We Wish You a Merry Christmas." Her eyes misted over. It was a beautiful night outside. Crisp and clear, the stars sparkled in the heavens. Inside the church, the pageant went off without a hitch. Hank's voice rang out clear and perfectly on pitch, leading the congregation in familiar songs from over the ages: "Silent Night," "Away in the Manger," "Joy to the World," "O Holy Night," and Jezabelle's favorite, "I Heard the Bells on Christmas Day."

The words to that song always reminded her that through the ages there had always been hate and sorrow, but love and peace could prevail. Yes, let the bells ring loud and strong. Unfortunately, there were no church bells here, but perhaps the new steeple would change that in the future.

Turning her attention to Mary and Joseph and baby Jesus, another tear escaped her eye. Seeing Santa kneeling at the manger stating, "I have finally found the true meaning of Christmas" totally got to her. The little children looked on in awe at Santa's words. Perhaps it had been a good idea to include Santa. Jezabelle wished she knew who he was. Maybe she too needed to believe.

Pastor Sifter gave the blessing, and turning to his wife, he gave the nod for Nellie to lead the pageant characters in a circle around the church, surrounding those who sat in the pews. The spotlight stayed on Joseph and Mary and baby Jesus, who remained in the manger at the front of the church. The lights faded, turning the church into darkness. When Nellie raised her hands, there was a small silence so deep a loud breath would have disturbed a sleeping baby. Each member of the cast switched on a small candle and began to sing "Let There Be Peace on Earth." Soon the congregation joined them.

Would there be peace with Ernest's death not solved? Would the mystery of his death and maybe the puzzle leave with the decorations and Santa and his elves? Were the Christmas holidays a part of the maze of deceit or just accidental timing?

Jezabelle gazed around the church as the lights came back on, and everyone scattered to give greetings to each other before rushing home to their Christmas Eve celebrations. She didn't see Disaster. He must have stayed hidden during the service. Santa made a beeline for the front door before anyone else noticed he had left. Jezabelle wondered if she should follow him.

"Jezzy, you are welcome to join Hanna and me for Christmas Eve dinner." Hank was standing at her side, looking over the crowd.

"I was looking for Rock. Is he coming to dinner?"

"No, he is still out of town," Hank answered.

"On Christmas Eve, he doesn't want to spend it with family?" she asked, referring to Hanna, who was Rock's wife."

Hank shrugged his shoulders.

"Thanks for the invitation, Hank, but I really want to spend Christmas Eve alone with a glass of wine. This holiday season has almost knocked me off my feet."

Hank eyed Jezabelle. "You're not spending Christmas Eve with your secret admirer? Or are you spinning me a tale so we don't find out about your secret tryst tonight?"

Jezabelle laughed and answered, "Why, Hank, you sound almost jealous. But no—no secret tryst with my admirer."

"There's Hanna. Are you sure you don't want to come with us?"

"No, I just want a quiet peaceful night. It's Christmas Eve and what better time for an evening of peace. See you in the morning at church services." Jezabelle gave a nod to Lizzy who was across the room.

"I must go. I have a gift for Lizzy, and I want to give it to her before she leaves. Have a wonderful night, and tell Hanna merry Christmas and Rock too if he shows up." Jezabelle quickly lifted up on her toes and gave him a peck on the cheek. Before Hank could say anything, she was weaving her way through the crowd in the church to Lizzy.

Hank muttered, "I guess that was my Christmas present. I can't wait to see what she gives Lizzy."

Chapter Thirty-Seven

Jezabelle sat in the quiet church. Seeing the others hadn't arrived, she took some time to contemplate all the information she had on the glass blocks. She chose a seat in the pew next to the carved nativity scene on the wall. It was dark with only the moon's beams shining through one of the stained glass windows. Wondering why the others hadn't arrived yet, she decided to look at the wall while she waited. She too had been late. It had been a long day, and she accidentally dozed off in her chair by her fireplace.

Shining the flashlight on the wall, she concentrated on the Three Wise Men. As she moved the light over their carved figures, she ran her other hand over the rough stone surface, stopping at the gifts they held in their hands. Putting her nose down to the gift on the Wise Man Melchior, whose name was carved into the base, she looked closely at the gift.

"Jezabelle!" A whispered voice sounded like a boom in the darkened church.

Jezabelle jumped and dropped her cell phone.

Snoop Steckle was behind her, and he reached down, grabbed the cell phone, and gave it back to her. "Shh! They can't know we are here." He grabbed her arm and pulled her down to the floor, hiding by the nearest pew.

"You almost caused the death of me. What are you doing here? You aren't supposed to be here. And why are we hiding?"

"From him."

"Him who?"

"Snodley."

"You're Snodley," Jezabelle reminded him.

"No… I have never been Snodley. Snodley's been Snoop but Snoop has never been Snodley."

"Did someone hit you over the head again?" Jezabelle asked.

"No. No one ever hit me over the head. They hit Snodley over the head and stuffed him into the box."

"Do you want to explain that to me? You really are making no sense."

"Shh!" Snoop reminded her.

Jezabelle started to stand up, and Snoop pulled her back down.

"He's here and he has your friends hostage until they give him information to the puzzle."

"Who's here?"

"Snodley. Okay, okay. I took a few weeks' vacation to somewhere warm, but I didn't want to miss out on anything, so I talked my brother Snodley into coming here and pretending to be me. He was in between hideouts, and he thought it was the perfect place to be. How was I to know that a puzzle would break after Ernest's death? I got back last night, and Snodley filled me in. Then he locked me in my bedroom in my house and took off. How did I know Snodley was greedy? Well, I did know, but I didn't think there was anything to be greedy about here in Brilliant."

Jezabelle looked at Snoop. "And why does he think there is now?"

"I told him about the last puzzle and the gold, so he is sure the new puzzle will lead to riches too."

"And how does he know about that?" Jezabelle's whisper was turning into an ire-filled question.

"I didn't tell him, I swear. He already knew something about Ernest the elf. He might have killed him, you know. He is a ruthless reporter and will do anything to get his story. He might have been hiding in Brilliant all along just waiting to find a time to get me to leave so he could pounce on the unsuspecting citizens of Brilliant."

"And why are we whispering and hiding behind this pew?" Jezabelle asked.

"I snuck out my window after he locked me in the bedroom and followed him. He has all your friends and the homeless man cornered behind a door you can't see over there on the other side of the church. He used a gun to get them to let him in."

"He has a gun? And he has my friends held hostage and you wasted all this time. He could have killed them by now, and no one would ever find them since very few people know about that room." Jezabelle stood up.

"We would have heard the shots," Snoop said.

"We wouldn't have heard the shots. It's a soundproof room." Jezabelle was yelling now. "And they can't hear us."

"You know about the room?"

Jezabelle ignored his question. "I think it's time to possibly bring the police in on this. There is a time and place for the police, and I think this is possibly the time and the place. You go outside and call Hank and the police. I will stay here and keep an eye on the wall to make sure if he has shot them he doesn't try to move the bodies." Jezabelle paced in the aisle.

Snoop's eyes widened so much Jezabelle could see the whites in the darkness.

"You think he shot them?"

Jezabelle pushed Snoop. "Get going."

"Yes... yes... I will, but I get the scoop, right? I get in on this."

"Just go!" Jezabelle yelled.

Chapter Thirty-Eight

Jezabelle waited until Snoop left the church. She walked across the church to the heart wall and tried to tiptoe high enough to see if she could look into the peek hole in the small heart. She couldn't reach it. Remembering Disaster said a person couldn't see in from outside, she still turned to look around to see if there was something she could stand on to test his truthfulness. With her back turned, she didn't notice the door silently opening.

Lizzy came out first. "Jezabelle, finally you got here."

Mr. Warbler, Disaster, Miranda, Hick, and Phoebe followed her. The last person out of the room was Snodley Steckle.

"You're not in danger? This is not Snoop. This is really Snodley who has pretended to be Snoop this entire time. Snoop told me he was holding you hostage in this room."

Snodley laughed. "I knew he would get out that window."

"He did take us hostage while we were waiting for you," a disgruntled Phoebe accused.

"Yes, but we quickly realized it was a fake gun," Hick noted. "It was an old cap gun from the fifties. I think the word Roy Rogers on the handle gave it away."

"You can't blame a guy for trying. I want part of the treasure," Snodley told them.

"We don't even know there is a treasure, but I have an idea," Jezabelle stated. "Does anyone know where George keeps his tools? I need a heavy hammer."

Miranda wrinkled her brow. "A hammer?"

"Yes, a hammer."

"I have it right here." George came in from the side door.

"What are you doing here, George?" Hick asked.

"I couldn't sleep because I wanted to get everything ready for Christmas morning services. I knew I had a few light bulbs out on the trees, little things like that. What are you all doing here? When I heard voices, I picked up my hammer when I was in my workshop downstairs, just in case I needed to defend myself. Since Disaster here kept me prisoner for a few days, I am always on the alert especially since Ernest was killed."

"Give me that hammer." Jezabelle reached for it. "We don't have much time. In fact, I am amazed Hank and his crew aren't here yet."

"You called the police?" Snodley's tone had changed from friendly to venomous.

"What's wrong with you?" Hick asked. "Mr. Fake Gunman."

Snodley tried to relax his body. "Nothing. Let's get on with it."

Jezabelle took off her coat and laid it on the floor. "Put the cubes there."

Disaster set them down. "Now what?"

"I'm going to turn on the lights. Since the police are coming and it is not unusual for me to be here at this time on Christmas morning, it's not going to hurt anything." George flipped the lights on.

Jezabelle continued. "What did the journal say? Something like the keys are with Balthazar, Melchior, and Gaspar. And we can't see the other side although they appear clear? I think it is kind of a strange magic trick or an unusual glass. Stand back."

Jezabelle held tight to the hammer and lifted her arm. She brought the hammer straight down on Balthazar. The glass shattered. She hit it again. A key flew out.

The bystanders gasped.

Mr. Warbler reached down and picked up the key. The key had the name Balthazar on it.

Jezabelle brought the hammer down hard on the other two blocks. A single key flew out of each of them.

Miranda grabbed both of them when they landed at her feet. "These two have the names of the other Wise Men. But what do we do with them?"

Jezabelle held out her hand. "I have an idea. I was investigating the wall before the real Snoop scared the life out of me."

Miranda and Mr. Warbler put the keys in her hand. Jezabelle weaved her way through the pews of the church to the wall with the nativity scene. The others followed.

She stopped at the wall and was about to explain when Pastor Sifter and Nellie came in from the back of the church. "We saw the lights and thought we better investigate. We called the police."

Jezabelle frowned. "Hank should have been here by now. I sent Snoop to call them."

"I called them. And you are right. They should have been here by now." Snoop joined the group.

"We're already here. We've been here all along." Hank appeared from the side door by the altar."

"HH, you mean you let all these people be in danger when Snodley kidnapped them?"

"We knew they weren't in any danger. We're the ones who gave Snodley the Roy Rodgers cap gun."

Phoebe marched up to Hank. "You knew all about this, and you let us think we were in danger. I will never flirt with you again." Phoebe turned and sat down in a pew.

"Well." Deputy Hanna Hardy joined the conversation. "We didn't know about the puzzle and the secret room until Santa here suspected somehow there was one when the homeless man kept disappearing. We suspected him in Ernest's death but couldn't ever catch up with him. Then Snodley started working with us too so we could nail him."

"Snodley is working with you?" Snoop exclaimed.

"And Jezabelle, apparently I haven't looked into your eyes enough because you didn't recognize me." Santa took off his hat and then his beard and peeled away a realistic-looking mask.

"Rock Stone, I knew I saw you out at my bird feeders one morning, but Hanna always said you were out of town," Mr. Warbler remarked.

"I am going to keep a better eye on you, Rock. We wanted you to help us with this cube puzzle thing. You are a chameleon." Jezabelle turned to Hank. "But why were you hiding here? We are almost going to solve the puzzle, and I thought you were going to do a dinner with Hanna? What would have happened if I would have accepted?"

Hank laughed. "Jezzy, I knew you wouldn't accept. I knew you were up to something. I've known you a long time. We knew somehow the church and the secret room you all discovered might be something to help us with our case. We wouldn't have known about any of it if you wouldn't have involved Snodley here."

Jezabelle held tightly to the keys in her hand and wondered if she should reveal her theory about the keys.

Nellie Sifter broke in, "I think my husband and I need to go home and get a little more sleep before Christmas morning services. We'll leave you to it since this involves murder."

Hanna moved to Nellie's side. "I think you should stay a while longer, Nellie."

"I'll have to get to work on preparing for Christmas services," George said. "I fixed those Christmas lights, but now I have to retrieve something out of my workshop."

Stick Straight moved out of the shadow of the doorway near them. "I think you should hear this, George."

"Hand me the hammer, Jezabelle." Hank reached out to take it.

"George, where did the blood come from on this hammer? Did you cut yourself, Jezabelle, when you were breaking the blocks?"

Jezabelle looked at her hands. "I don't think so."

"George, if I take this hammer in to be tested, I would guess it would match Ernest the elf's blood. Am I right?" Hank questioned.

Nellie began to cry.

Hank turned to Nellie. "And if I moved the baptismal font a little"—he moved toward the front of the church by the baptismal font—"I would guess if we had a team come and check this, we would find small specks of blood from Ernest. Am I right Nellie?"

Pastor Sifter turned to his wife. "You killed Ernest the elf? Nellie, I can't believe this."

Nellie began to sob. "I didn't, or if I did, I didn't mean to." She began to cry harder.

George sighed. "Yes, that is Ernest the elf's blood on my hammer. But I didn't think I was the one who killed him. I hit him, but he must have got up and left, so he was alive after I hit him."

The Discombobulated Decipherers simultaneously gasped, the noise echoing in the empty church.

George sat down. "How did you figure this out?"

"I told him. I was staying at Snoop's house and found some notes Snoop wrote," Snodley Steckle admitted.

Nellie, finally calmer, started talking. "The night Ernest the elf was killed, I woke up and looked out my window and saw lights in the church. We had choir practice that night, so I thought I left the lights on. Since I couldn't sleep anyway, I thought I would run over and turn them out." She took a deep breath before continuing. "When I got here, I saw Ernest the elf. When he saw me, he lifted the baptismal font and put something underneath. I confronted him, and then he came on to me and made sexual advances. I pushed him, and he fell back and hit his head on the baptismal font. The font tipped over. I felt bad so I leaned down to help him, and then he attacked me again. That's when George came out of nowhere and hit him with the hammer. I, for some reason, grabbed the pages he hid under the baptismal font and ran out."

George continued the story. "I saw Ernest attacking Nellie and then go down and hit the font and Nellie running out. Ernest tried to get up and run after her, so I had the hammer in my hand, and I hit him and he fell again. I knew she was upset, so I ran after her and calmed her down. I sent her home and then went back to tend to Ernest, planning on calling an ambulance, but Ernest was gone. We both thought he was still alive and got scared and left."

"Until the next morning when Miranda found his body in the town square wrapped in Christmas lights," Nellie continued.

"Why didn't you come forward?" Pastor Sifter addressed his wife. "Why didn't you tell me? We would have figured this out."

"I was scared. You are always telling me to not go to the church in the middle of the night, and now Ernest was dead and I might have killed him even though it was him who attacked me," Nellie explained.

"And now it's your turn. Why don't you tell us how this all ends, Snoop? Isn't that why you took a vacation?" Hank turned to Snoop Steckle.

Snoop turned white. "How did you figure it out?"

"It wasn't easy," Hank answered. "Were you protecting Nellie too?"

Snoop hung his head. "I'm sorry, Nellie. I was only trying to keep you out of trouble. I thought you and George killed him. I saw it all because I was watching, trying to get a story. I had been following Ernest because it appeared he was looking for something. I always saw him looking for something in places he shouldn't be. I followed him into the church the night before and saw him chisel the cube from the wall. I followed him out and lost track of him. He must have somehow had to ditch the cube and hide it in the chipped step of the church as he was leaving out the front door. So when he went back into the church the next night, I was there too. I saw him attack you, and I was going to step out and help when George did. When you ran out and George ran after you, I took matters into my own hands. I have an infatuation with you, and I didn't want to see anything happen to you so I lifted Elfy—it wasn't hard because he was little—and I took him out to be found in the square."

"You wrapped him in Christmas lights?" Phoebe's astonished tone wasn't lost on the others.

"I... ah... didn't. He kind of flopped, hit the lights, and they came down, and as I was trying to get him loose, they wrapped around him. It was a fluke. But I didn't kill him, he was already dead," Snoop continued.

"And then he left town, giving me this story that he needed a vacation and I could become him for a few weeks, never letting me in on the fact he could be an accessory to murder," Snodley answered. "I knew the jig was up when I got stuffed into the box, so I talked to Hank. I wasn't a crackpot reporter for nothing."

"Does that mean he gets the story and I don't?" Snoop asked.

194 • JULIE SEEDORF

"I think you shouldn't worry about the story but how much time you might have to spend at the police station while we go over this again. You need to come along too, Nellie. And you too, George." Hank turned to Pastor Sifter. "I know it's Christmas and it's almost morning and services need to begin at ten a.m. It does sound like self-defense to me for Nellie."

"That's what it was for me too. I was just protecting Nellie," Snoop added.

"Unfortunately, it is not that simple," Hank informed him. "Ernest didn't die from the blow on the head, he froze to death."

"Let's get you three down to the station and get this sorted out. I would suggest the rest of you go home and get some rest so we can all have a merry Christmas."

The officers and suspects left the church.

"Well, Rock"—Jezabelle addressed the undercover detective—"where's your ho, ho, ho, now? How can we have a merry Christmas after all this?"

Chapter Thirty-Nine

The Discombobulated Decipherers watched the others leave. They were the only ones left in the church with Snodley and Pastor Sifter going to the police station too to be of aid to Snoop and Nellie. Rock followed them after putting another piece to the puzzle and apologizing to Mr. Warbler for his fall on the church steps. Rock had left the practice early to crush some more of the steps to see if there was anything more Ernest has hidden there, thinking no one would notice if the steps crumbled some more because of the cold.

"Are you all going home like Chief Hardy suggested?" Disaster had been silent until now, trying not to draw attention to himself. "Apparently, they aren't too interested in me anymore."

Jezabelle shook her head. "That is kind of strange. They didn't say a thing about finding the secret room or why you are living there or anything else about our puzzle."

"Well, the murder's solved. Let's not look a gift horse in the mouth," Phoebe exclaimed.

Miranda stepped forward. "It is kind of strange that Snodley left, but I guess Hank was just trying to draw Snoop and the truth out."

Hick interjected, "And he left us here. That is unusual."

"He did and instead of questioning his decision, we better figure this puzzle out before something more happens." Jezabelle opened her hand with the keys.

"This is the strangest Christmas Eve and morning I have ever spent. It makes me miss Santa presents under the tree," Phoebe mused.

"Were your Santa presents strange?" Mr. Warbler asked.

"Only when Sigfried talked to Santa before I did," Phoebe answered.

Jezabelle moved to the nativity wall. "I noticed a little slit carved into the gifts the Wise Men hold. Do you suppose they incorporated a lock in the walls many years ago in the sculptures?" Looking at her hand, she pulled out the key to Balthazar.

Miranda held out her hand. "Let me try it. I am good at picking locks, so I should be good at tiny keys."

"You can pick locks?" Hick asked in admiration.

"It's part of being a mystery writer. I wanted it to be authentic in my books, and to do that, I thought learning to pick locks would keep it authentic because I had experienced it," Miranda answered as she stuck the key in the gift.

"Does that mean you kill people too so you can be authentic in your book?" Phoebe said sarcastically.

"Look, it turned and now the gift is loose." She pushed the square gift, and it moved inward. "Try the next key."

Jezabelle took the next key and put it into Melchior while handing the last key to Mr. Warbler.

Both keys turned and the gifts pushed inward when Mr. Warbler and Jezabelle touched the square stone.

"Now what. Nothing happened," Warbler stated.

"Turn the locks again so the gifts come back into place," Jezabelle ordered.

The two followed her instructions as the others watched.

"Now turn and push all at the same time at the count of three. One. Two. Three." Jezabelle held her breath to see what would happen.

As the three pushed, they could hear something unlatch.

Hick came forward. "That sounded like another lock unlatching. Let me in there." He examined the Three Wise Men. "You can see the three are all connected as they are next to one another, but the edges that surround the three seem to be deeper. Maybe it's like the heart wall on the other side of the church." He gave a big push, and the Three Wise Men on the wall slipped backward and left an opening on either side.

Hick was the first one through. They heard him let out a whistle in amazement. "There's a room, but turn on your cell phone lights. It's dark in here."

The others squeezed through the opening.

"It's a little girl's playroom." Miranda took in the small play castle in the far corner decorated in pink and white.

"It's been locked up in time." Lizzy ran her hand over the princess chair in the corner, feeling the dust coming off the white wood.

"Is there a light?" Hick asked, feeling the walls.

"I don't think so." Jezabelle shone her light around the ceiling, which was painted in blue with white fluffy clouds.

"A playroom without any windows?" Mr. Warbler wondered.

"This is a room under the closed bell tower that we could never access," Jezabelle answered.

"It must have been Belle's playroom. A playroom in a church—that's unique." Miranda continued on around the room, examining its contents. "Look, here are some partially burned candles. Everything seems as if it was left as it was. It was sealed tight so nothing disintegrated.

"Then it must have been used, but I thought the story that Nellie gave the architect said they didn't finish it and then sealed it up when Broderick's daughter died," Lizzy thought out loud.

Disaster spoke, startling the others as they had forgotten he was with them because he had been unusually quiet. "This was my family," he said in awe. "And it wasn't the end of their story or Broderick wouldn't have left the puzzle or the journal so it could be found later in history."

"So this is the treasure that we have been looking for?" Phoebe asked. "It hardly seems that interesting that it would be a big find someday."

"Look, there's a stone stairway hidden behind the castle." Hick pushed the wooden castle aside.

"Since you figured out how to get into this room Jezabelle, you should be first up this stairway but maybe I should test it to make sure it is safe and not crumbled," Hick suggested.

Jezabelle moved him out of the way. "I'm lighter than you. I'll go first and Disaster can come with me since this was his family. We'll call down to let you know if you should follow. It might lead to a dead end or just be a small space. Come on Disaster."

Jezabelle moved her light from her phone to examine the steps and the walls. "It looks safe." She started up the steps with Disaster following her.

The steps seemed to go on forever, but then a bell tower was high. At the end of the steps was a big open space, and what was in the middle of the big open space left Jezabelle and Disaster speechless for a moment. Their lights from their phones revealed it sparkling in the night.

Disaster found his voice first. "Oh my."

"It leaves me breathless." Jezabelle finally spoke.

"Are you two alive up there?" Lizzy's voice could be heard from the bottom of the stairs.

"We are, and you all need to see this. We found the treasure." Jezabelle spoke loudly so they could hear.

When the others reached the top of the steps and moved into the room, they let out a gasp.

"Is that what I think it is, or am I seeing things in the darkness?" Phoebe asked.

"How can this be? I do need to write about this." Miranda moved forward to lightly touch the object."

"Is it breakable?" Mr. Warbler chirped.

Hick was moving around the walls. "I wish there were some light so we could see it better."

"How did they get this up here through that narrow staircase?" Jezabelle pondered.

"Miranda, come and help me. I think this bell tower was open at one time, and it feels like something is on the sides covering the openings. Everyone direct your flashlights on this wall. I can feel the edges of something."

"So can I," Miranda added. "Let's see if these window coverings slide sideways." She started pushing.

"They can't slide. There is nowhere for them to slide sideways to because it appears this covering goes all the way around the tower." Hick informed the group.

Disaster was examining the ceiling. "It looks like there are tracks of some sort on the ceiling. If you notice on the stone over the windows there is a track that curves right into the curved ceiling." He showed them with his light.

Mr. Warbler backed up closer to the door to the stairwell. The others heard a crash.

"Warby, Warby, are you all right?" Lizzy shone her light onto Mr. Warbler lying prone over some kind of square mechanical gadget to the left of the doorway.

"I'm fine." Warbler lifted himself up off the contraption that had caused his fall. "What is this?"

Disaster moved by Mr. Warbler and examined the box. "It's a gearbox with different cranks and gears. It's preserved pretty well because there is no rust."

"What is it for?" Phoebe asked.

"Let's find out," Disaster said as touched one handle that would move the gear when cranking it.

The other's watched as he stopped and started. "It's a little stiff from nonuse." He gave it another crank, and soon the gears began moving. They heard a shutter from the stone over on the wall, and soon the panels began lifting and gliding to the ceiling.

"We know what this gear does. This has to be a heavy-duty moving machine to move that stone," Disaster commented.

"Look... and there is a fake stone on the outside, and that is what we have been seeing all these years instead of one solid tower. I wonder if we can take them out." Hick tapped on the fake stone and saw it was sitting in grooves carved into place in the wall. He lifted them out, letting the early morning air into the tower. "I guess this was to protect it and hide its presence from observers."

What about the gear next to it?" Miranda asked.

Disaster moved to the next gear. As he began to turn the gear, the song "Jesus Loves Me" began to play in the tone of chimes like a bell. He stopped cranking, and the music stopped.

"This is amazing." Jezabelle moved forward to touch the crystal bell in the middle of the tower. "The bell can't toll, but they fixed it so there would still be chimes. Without electricity, it was the way they made it work."

Miranda examined the crystal bell more closely with her cell phone light. "Do you suppose this is real crystal?"

"And why as a bell in a church tower. Certainly it would break from the wind and the weather," Lizzy pointed out.

"I'm sure that is why the protection on the windows. But perhaps when they sealed up the tower, they added the heavy stone on the inside so no one would ever find out the secret of the tower," Jezabelle surmised.

"This must be worth a fortune," Phoebe guessed.

"And it should be your treasure, Disaster, if you can prove you are who you are," Lizzy added.

"We need to put the windows back. Where do we go from here?" Jezabelle pondered what to do next.

"We have a suggestion."

The others turned, startled at a voice that hadn't been part of the conversation. Hank and Rock Stone stood in the doorway of the tower room.

Chapter Forty

The chorus of "Joy to the World" filled the Brilliant church on Christmas morning at the end of the service. Jezabelle needed the lively song to keep her eyes open since she hadn't had any sleep, the events of the early morning keeping her awake.

She looked around the church to see all the Discombobulated Decipherers had made it. Hank and Hanna and Rock sat next to her, with Hick and Miranda sharing the pew in front of them. Lizzy and Mr. Warbler were farther back on the same side of the church by the door so they could be the first out. Sigfried Shepherd sat behind Phoebe. Phoebe was trying to ignore him as their voices blended together in song. Disaster sat in the front row dressed in his Christmas best, having discarded his homeless persona. Her musings were interrupted when the song ended and Pastor Sifter asked the congregation to sit down for a moment before they left to their Christmas celebrations.

"As you may have all heard, there was quite the commotion here last night. I, along with the police department and the Discombobulated Decipherers—in case you haven't heard of them, you can be updated about their organization later—decided we needed to address the issues at hand. I feel the best person to explain some of this is Hank Hardy. Hank, I turn the pulpit over to you."

Jezabelle watched as Hank made his way to the altar.

"First of all, I will have to tell you that Ernest the elf's demise was somewhat of an accident. The details will have to be sorted out by the courts at a later date. I will say this—it appears Nellie Sifter was defending herself and George was protecting her. I doubt whether there will be any charges filed there. Unfortunately, the verdict is still out upon further investigation for Snoop Steckle. Since it's Christmas and Snoop has been a part of this community for the past eight years and has an impeccable record except for snooping, he has been released on his own recognizance to await trial. I encourage you all to reserve judgment on his guilt or innocence. Having said that, it is also because of the Discombobulated Decipherers that we have solved another puzzle. I would like to introduce you to Disaster Brilliant Darling—and yes, that is his name. He is a direct descendant of the Brilliant brothers who built our town. He came to town looking for answers. Disaster, I'll turn it over to you."

Disaster approached the microphone. "Ernest was the handyman for my parents. He found a journal in their attic, but he only took a few pages and part of an architectural drawing. Nellie found those pages the night Ernest was killed, which explains that when the church was being built, Broderick Brilliant's daughter died. Little Belle loved church bells and their chimes, and so they were building a special bell tower for her. When she died, they, in their grief, sealed up the tower so no one could access it. That is why this church does not have a bell tower, only a semblance of one outside. I think Jezabelle Jingle should finish the story because we have a Christmas gift for you. Jezabelle?"

Jezabelle was not expecting to be called to explain anything that happened, so she hesitated to get up, but Lizzy got up, came forward, and grabbed her arm to lead her to the front of the church.

When she got to the microphone, she collected her thoughts before speaking. "Yes, well… it so happens when the Brilliant Brother built this church, he also made it a puzzle with secret rooms and secret doors and the discombobulated ones along with Disaster put two and two together. I don't want to spoil the surprise, but I will tell you that the little girl, whom the tower was built for, loved music, loved the church, and she loved Christmas and the reason for Christmas, Jesus's birth. We also know from the room we found built in this church for her to play in that she was well loved, and her father wanted a legacy that would live forever. Though the dream died when she died, he had enough wisdom to know time would pass, and those that came after him might need a message of hope in this world we live in. We were blessed enough to be the ones that found it. I will ask you all to step outside in the beautiful snow-frosted square kissed by sunshine today. Look to the tower, and I hope this surprise will fill you with peace on earth this Christmas Day."

Jezabelle watched as the congregation filed out of the church into the sunshine and the town square. She nodded to Hank and Disaster as they moved to the side of the church, turned the keys, and started the journey to the bell tower room. Once she saw they were in place, she hurried outside to join the rest of the Discombobulated Decipherers.

The crowd waited, all eyes on the bell tower. Their murmurs could be heard throughout the square. The murmurs turned to gasps of awe as the door of the bell tower room was opened and the large crystal bell could be seen hanging in the tower, the sun glinting off the crystals, giving a feel of celestial radiance. The chimes began playing "Let There Be Peace on Earth." And soon the voices of those in the square accompanied the chimes, some moved to tears that a little girl born so long ago and living such a short life would bring peace to their hearts on this special day.

Epilogue

Lizzy let out a sigh of relief. "Finally I am going to meet this mysterious man in your life. I can't believe you haven't even told me, your best friend, who he is."

Jezabelle giggled. "Lizzy, I can't believe you haven't figured it out."

"I think the others are a little put out that we didn't ask them over for New Year's Eve. Hopefully, Warby didn't say anything."

"You swore him to secrecy, and he is the best secret keeper ever. You know he kept his secret of being Marco Renaldo from us for years and still wouldn't have told us if we hadn't stumbled upon the secret. Besides, he has this thing for you."

Lizzy giggled. "You think? I hope so. That's why I decided we should have this quiet evening, just the four of us. Warby and I and you and— You haven't told me his name."

Jezabelle gave Lizzy a sly smile. "I haven't, have I? I never did tell the group that the glass block in the bank window fit with the other places the blocks were hidden. Apparently, that wasn't the original window. The original window was a colored block that formed a nativity scene. But for some reason they had to fix the window, and they put in the clear block but left the remaining clear blocks from the edges of the original window. That is how Melchior stayed in the bank window. It was something about one of the bank presidents over the years feeling they shouldn't have Mary and Joseph year round on a bank window even if it was a basement window."

A knock at the door interrupted Jezabelle's explanation.

Lizzy checked her hair in the dining room mirror above the buffet and made a minor adjustment to the dinner table she had decorated for New Year's before answering the door.

"For you, Lizzy." Mr. Warbler handed Lizzy a bouquet of red roses.

"Why, Warby, you didn't have to bring me flowers." Lizzy blushed.

"A rose for a rose," Warby countered.

Jezabelle rolled her eyes and went to the door as she saw her guest had arrived.

Lizzy's mouth dropped open when she saw who was at the door.

Mr. Warbler chuckled. "Apparently, we are not as good of sleuths as we thought. Hi, Hank."

"Hank? Hank is your secret admirer?" Lizzy squealed.

"Sit down, Hank. Let's all sit down before Lizzy falls down," Jezabelle suggested.

"I just don't understand why you have kept this secret," Lizzy scolded.

"Later, Lizzy, I'll help you with the food." Jezabelle exited into the kitchen and came out with the appetizer of sausage stuffed mushrooms and bacon-wrapped pineapple shrimp. Lizzy gave the bottle of champagne to Hank to open.

After the drinks were poured, Lizzy asked, "Should we make a toast?"

"Before we do that, I have something I want to do first," Hank answered.

Jezabelle squirmed in her chair. "Maybe I should make sure our dinner isn't burning." She started to get up.

Hank stopped her. "Jezabelle, do you still have those rings you received that night in the church from your secret admirer?" He winked at her.

Lizzy's eyes became wide as saucers. Mr. Warbler snuck his hand over to Lizzy's and gently held it, anticipating something to come.

Jezabelle got up and moved to the stand in her living room. Opening the drawer, she pulled out the box with the rings and handed it to Hank.

He opened the box and took out the rings. Looking into Jezabelle's eyes, he took her hand. "Jezabelle, would you marry me again?"

Lizzy choked when she heard the words "again."

Jezabelle looked into Hank's eyes and said, "Those were the best two weeks of my life. That the rest of my life would be like those two weeks, yes, Hank, I will marry you again."

Hank put the engagement ring on Jezabelle's finger. He turned to Lizzy and Mr. Warbler as he picked up his champagne glass. "To the love of my life."

Just as he said those words, a flash came from the doorway, and then Hanna, Rock, Phoebe, Miranda, and Hick spilled into the room declaring, "Happy New Year."

Jezabelle gasped. "What are you all doing here?"

"We knew something was up," Rock said. "Hanna saw her dad pull up, and she saw Phoebe peeking out behind her window curtain. Hick and Miranda were sitting on her porch, staring at your house, Jezabelle. We knew Lizzy and Warbler weren't at their houses. So we put our heads together and decided to crash the party."

Hanna stared at Jezabelle's hand. "You're engaged? You're engaged?" Then seeing her father sitting next to Jezabelle, she said, "To my dad?"

"Hanna, there's something we haven't told any of you." Hank stood up. "I have known Jezabelle since high school. She was friends with your mother. Your mother and I were each other's first loves. We went together in high school, but we broke up when your mother went off to college. She decided she wanted to spread her wings and that I wasn't the one for her. Jezabelle and I left Brilliant and went to the University of Minnesota, and the first month or so we spent a lot of time together, being alone in a big city and all, and on a school campus. It felt like instantly we fell in love. It was a surprise to us after knowing each other and being friends for years. We eloped to Las Vegas and started a life together. We kept it secret because we felt our parents wouldn't understand since it was such a short time we were together before marrying and we still had college to finish. We were going to tell everyone when we graduated in four or five years."

Hank looked around the room at the astonished faces, including that of his daughter. "But two weeks after we got married, your mother contacted me. She was pregnant with you. Jezabelle loved your mother, and she put her and your interests first, and we decided we should part and I should marry your mother."

Hanna asked, "Did Mom know?"

Jezabelle stood up and took Hanna's hand. "No, we never told her. It would only have made her wonder if Hank really loved her, and he did. He was with her a long time before we decided we were in love. That was the best two weeks of my life."

Hank continued, "We kept this all secret, not because we are ashamed of our relationship, but because we wanted to be sure, plus Jezabelle keeps coming up with all these crazy puzzle groups, and it drove me crazy because it kept getting in the way of our spending time together."

Another flash went off, this time outside the window.

"What the heck?" Jezabelle stated, peering out the window into the darkened night. "I thought Snoop was done with his snooping, at least until his court date."

"Oh, it's Snodley. He decided to stick around and take Snoop's place until after the trial. I guess your engagement will be on the front page of the Brilliant Times Chronicle tomorrow."

Hanna walked over to Jezabelle and took her hand and then took her dad's hand and joined them together. "Jezabelle, will you marry us?"

The End

Recipes

Coming soon to the Brilliant Bistro

WORK-IN-PROGRESS CUPCAKES

My granddaughter Maggie and I enjoy making recipes from scratch. These cupcakes have cranberry juice, taffy, honey, and various toppings made of different gooey substances. We haven't gotten them quite perfected yet. We also decided we wanted to make them gluten-free, so we are back to experimenting. Maggie is the baker. I am only into cheesecakes.

We will let you experiment too. If you come up with a winner all on your own from scratch, send it to me and I may choose some to post on my website and give you credit. Jezabelle, who has the final say, will be picky, and we will make it to test it out. It has to be your very own recipe and have the following ingredients in them. We decided to call these Work-in-Progress Cupcakes.

Ingredients:
2 ¾ cup cake flour
3 ½ tsp. baking soda
1 tsp. salt
¼ cup cream cheese and a little splash of cranberry juice, microwaved to melt

½ cup honey
2 tbsp. vegetable oil
½ stick butter
¼ cup sugar
3 eggs
¼ melted taffy

Blend all ingredients. Bake at 350 until a toothpick comes out clean. (LOL. It never will.)

Frosting:
2 oz. cream cheese
¾ cup whipping cream
1 cup marshmallow cream
½ cup powdered sugar

Whip together.

Try this recipe at your own risk. It actually wasn't bad, just too moist. We wanted to experiment with what all we could throw together and see what turns out. We have since been working on perfecting this, and it is coming together better than we'd thought, but it will be gluten-free. Look for it in the next book, unless of course we use yours.

LEMON LOVE NOTES

Jezabelle and I would like to thank Gladys Johanson and her family for letting us use her recipe for Lemon Love Notes in the Brilliant Bistro. Gladys celebrated her 100th birthday on October 19, 2017. She fed 14 children with her fabulous cooking. Thank you for sharing love through your baking.

Ingredients:
½ cup butter
1 cup flour
¼ cup powdered sugar
Mix together – pat in 9" pan. Bake 15 minutes at 350 degrees. Cool.
2 tbsp. lemon juice
1 grated lemon rind
2 eggs beaten
1 cup sugar
2 tbsp. flour
½ tsp. baking powder

Blend together ingredients, pour over baked crust. Bake 25 minutes at 350 degree. Cool.

Frosting:
¾ cup powdered sugar
1 tbsp. butter
1 ½ tsp. milk
Mix well. Frost lemon bars.

PEANUT BUTTER CUP CHEESECAKE

Recipe Courtesy of *Taste of Home* Magazine

Yield 12 – 14 Servings
1 ¼ cup Graham Cracker Crumbs
¼ cup sugar
¼ cup cream-filled chocolate sandwich cookies
6 Tablespoons butter, melted
¾ cup creamy peanut butter

Filling
3 packages (3 ounces each) cream cheese softened
1 cup sugar
1 cup (8 ounces) sour cream
1 ½ tsps. vanilla extract
3 eggs lightly beaten
1 cup hot fudge ice cream topping, divided
6 peanut butter cups cut into small wedges

Directions:
1.   In a large bowl, combine the cracker crumbs, sugar, cookie crumbs and butter. Press onto the bottom and 1 inch up the sides of a greased 9-inch springform pan. Place on a baking sheet.
2.   Bake at 350 degrees for 5-7 minutes or until set. Cook on a wire rack. In a microwave-safe bowl, heat peanut butter on high for 30 seconds or until softened. Spread over crust to within 1 in. of edges.
3.   In a large bowl, beat cream cheese and sugar until smooth. Beat in sour cream and vanilla. Add eggs; beat on low speed until combined. Pour 1 cup into a bowl; set aside. Pour remaining filling over peanut butter layer.
4.   In a microwave, heat ¼ cup fudge topping on high for 30 seconds or until thin; fold into reserved cream cheese mixture. Carefully pour over filling; cut through with knife to swirl.

5.   Return pan to baking sheet. Bake at 350 degrees for 55-65 minutes or until center is almost set. Cool on a wire rack for 10 minutes. Carefully run a knife around edge of pan to loosen, cool 1 hour longer.

6.   Microwave remaining topping for 30 seconds or until warmed; spread over cheesecake. Garnish with peanut butter cups. Refrigerate overnight. Refrigerate leftovers.

https://www.tasteofhome.com/recipes/
peanut-butter-cup-cheesecake

I always dreamed of becoming an actress or an author. The adults in my life would call them "pipe dreams." Imagination always got me in trouble, and people didn't take me too seriously. Add that to the fact that I had blond hair, and the title "ditsy blonde" could be heard in teasing. As an adult, I married, raised my children, and settled into careers that were respected, finally becoming a computer technician and owning my own computer business, selling and repairing computers. People took me seriously and gave me respect for my knowledge of computers. During those years, I used my creativity in my children's activities and volunteer positions, writing Christmas programs and Lenten services for our church. I hid the poems and writing I wrote as a teenager and young adult and put them out of my mind because a writing career was a dream. I believed what I had been told, that it was a pipe dream.

During my life, I was an avid reader, starting out with Trixie Beldon, Nancy Drew, and expanding my world with romances, mysteries, inspirational reading, and gritty crime stories. I was in awe of the talent of the authors. In 2005 I took the chance of sending my thoughts to an area newspaper, and they accepted me as a columnist for their paper. I have been writing my column Something About Nothing since then. I write about anything that comes to mind, sometimes meaningful and sometimes fluffy and about nothing, but just silly.

In 2011, during an illness that laid me low, I began to write a story on my blog about a silly fictional town in Minnesota with an older woman character that defied our idea of old age. Each day I would wake up with a new chapter in my head. This story got me out of my illness and back into the world along with the help of good doctors and many encouraging friends. One day, I was reading a book that sounded somewhat like the book I wrote. It was a cozy mystery. I didn't know what a cozy mystery was. I looked it up, found the publisher, sent in a query letter, and got accepted after a few changes to my book. Being accepted for publication by Cozy Cat Press began a new life for me. I now have five books out in the Fuchsia, Minnesota, series, two books out in the Granny Is In Trouble series for kids and my first book published with some of my earlier columns.

In 2017 I published a picture book about friendship for children and young-at-heart adults.

I feel truly blessed in my life. A few years ago, I quit my computer business to write full time, and I hope to have many more book ideas swirling around in my mind. I now know I need to have faith in myself and listen to the whispers in my heart. Creativity and imagination are a blessing, and I encourage others to never give up on their dream, no matter their age.

–Julie Seedorf

Fuchsia, Minnesota Series
Granny Hooks a Crook
Granny Skewers a Scoundrel
Granny Snows a Sneak
Granny Forks a Fugitive
Granny Pins a Pilferer

Brilliant, Minnesota Series
The Penderghast Puzzle Protectors
The Discombobulated Decipherers

Granny's in Trouble Series
Whatchamacallit? Thingamajig?
Snicklefritz

Stand-Alones
Two Little Girls
Something About Nothing

Anthologies and Group Mysteries
We Go On: Charity Anthology for Veterans
published by Kiki Howel
Chasing the Codex
published by Cozy Cat Press

Websites
  http://julieseedorf.com
  http://sprinklednotes.com
  http://thecozycatchronicles.com
  http://www.facebook.com/julie.seedorf.author
  http://www.twitter.com/julieseedorf
  http://www.instagram.com/julie_seedorf

My column
  http://www.albertleatribune.com/category/opinion/columns/
something-about-nothing/

Made in the USA
Columbia, SC
17 June 2018